# *Deadly Drive*

### David Patneaude

Albert Whitman & Company
Morton Grove, Illinois

Library of Congress Cataloging-in-Publication Data

Patneaude, David.
Deadly drive / by David Patneaude.
p. cm.
Summary: On Whidbey Island, Washington, fourteen-year-old Casey has two
goals—to become an excellent basketball player like her mother was, and
to find the hit-and-run driver who injured her and killed
her mother nine years earlier.
ISBN 13: 978-0-8075-0844-2 (hardcover)
ISBN 13: 978-0-8075-0845-9 (paperback)
[1. Basketball—Fiction. 2. Interpersonal relations—Fiction. 3. Wounds and
injuries—Fiction. 4. Single-parent families—Fiction. 5. Mothers
and daughters—Fiction. 6. Whidbey Island (Wash.)—Fiction.] I. Title.
PZ7.P2734De 2005 [Fic]—dc22 2004019916

Design by Carol Gildar.

*For information about Albert Whitman & Company,*
*please visit our web site at www.albertwhitman.com.*

*For my treasured brothers and sisters—*
*Mike, Susan, Rick, Kate, Jim, and Mark—*
*and long-ago, never-a-dull-moment laughs*
*around the dinner table.*
*Thanks for the memories and inspiration.*

David Patneaude was born in St. Paul, Minnesota, but he has lived in the Seattle, Washington, area since he was six. He graduated from the University of Washington and served in the U.S. Navy.

He is the author of *Someone Was Watching*, winner of the South Dakota Prairie Pasque Award and the Utah Children's Book Award; *The Last Man's Reward*, included on the New York Public Library's 1997 Books for the Teen Age; *Dark Starry Morning: Stories of This World and Beyond*; *Framed in Fire*; *Haunting at Home Plate*; and *Colder Than Ice*. His books have been included on more than twenty state young readers' lists.

David lives in Woodinville, Washington, with his wife, Judy, and their two children, Jaime and Jeff. In his spare time he enjoys running, coaching, exploring the outdoors, and reading.

# ❧ Contents ❧

# ~ *1* ~

# New Girl on the Island

The first thing I noticed when I got home from school was the moving truck across the street. Just the truck, no new neighbors. Yet.

Sorting through the mail, I hurried inside and upstairs to my bedroom. Through my window I saw moving guys coming out of the house. I changed into an old T-shirt and shorts and my broken-in Nikes, grabbed my basketball, and headed back down.

Was the population of fourteen-year-old girls on my block really going to double? I had to find out. I'd watch for the new kid while I practiced hoops.

And maybe concentrating on two things at once would get my mind off what I'd been thinking about since my alarm had gone off that morning.

It was May fifteenth, the beginning of mysterious-envelope season. Would another puzzling package arrive in the next few days, the way one had for as long as I could remember?

I started my routine: stretching, ball-handling and flexibility drills, bouncing passes off the garage door. As usual, I thought about working on my right hand, but barely spent any time at it. I took shots, layups first, then out, out, out, to my raggedy three-point line and beyond. I had to build up my wrist strength. I was tall for an eighth-grader, but not for a basketball player. Not yet, anyway. If I was going to play in high school and college, I needed an outside shot.

And I wanted to play in high school and college. I wanted to be the best girl basketball player ever to grow up in Island County, the best in the whole state.

I wanted to be as good as my mom.

Across the street the movers were wrestling a refrigerator down the truck's ramp. A silver-colored car now sat, unoccupied, in the driveway.

I kept working. The sun had broken out, and for spring in the little Whidbey Island town of Langley, Washington, it was warm.

Now the guys lurched from the truck with a white-and-pink dresser. A girl's dresser. I didn't see a girl, but a thin black woman paced the yard, giving directions.

She saw me looking and waved. I waved back. She smiled, friendly. I returned to my routine.

The woman went into the house and returned with cans of pop, and the movers took a break. I kept working. I went to the free throw line for my hundred.

I started off slow—six of ten—then made five in a row. The next six went through so cleanly that they just kissed the garage door and caromed back, like I had one of those automatic return machines. I thought I couldn't miss, but the next one clanged off the rim. Seventeen of twenty-two.

"I was wondering when you'd miss."

I turned, expecting to see the woman. Instead, a girl stood at the edge of my driveway. She smiled the woman's smile. She was the woman's color but a shade lighter. "I miss all the time," I said.

The ball rolled to her. She scooped it up and underhanded it to me. "Nice ball."

"It was a present—for my fourteenth birthday."

"A little birdie—actually, the real estate lady— told me you were fourteen."

"That same birdie told my dad that you—or your sister, maybe—are fourteen, too."

"As of last September," she said. "And I don't have a sister."

"My birthday's in March," I said.

"Final Four month."

"I'm gonna play in it someday." I don't know why I said that. I really hoped to play in the Final Four when I got to college, but why was

I saying it out loud to this stranger?

"You, too?"

"I'm Casey," I said. "Casey Wilde." I twist-swirled the ball onto my first finger and tapped it to keep it spinning. The girl's smile stayed, but her wide brown eyes narrowed.

"My birthday's September twenty-first."

"Huh," I said, lobbing back the ball.

She caught it on her finger and swiped at it. In no time it was a blur. "That's a clue," she said, "for my name."

"Really?" I wasn't good at puzzles. But maybe the twenty-first was related to the alphabet, like those codes you use when you're a kid playing spy. Maybe her name had something to do with the twenty-first letter. I counted. "Your name begins with a U?"

"What?" She frown-smiled.

I shrugged. "Sometimes I leap ahead."

"You better get yourself a safety net, girl." She flipped the ball to her other hand, where it touched down on her finger, still rotating. I'd never even tried that.

I kept thinking. She moved closer. She was about my height, maybe an inch shorter, and my shape, mostly, but she had muscles in her shoulders and arms where I was trying to develop something besides my ugly scar.

"What happens on September twenty-first, most years?"

4

"Fall," I blurted. "Fall starts."

Her smile widened. "You're warm."

She tossed the ball back to me. I had the answer. "Autumn."

"You're smart, country girl," she said. "I'm Autumn Hopkins. Some people call me Hops."

Hops. How high could she fly? "Wanna shoot around?" I asked, checking out her clothes: nice sandals, white shorts, pink tank-top. She wore sparkling post earrings high and low in each ear. I fingered my ear, naked and drab, reminded that I'd left my earrings on the dresser that morning.

"I'll go change." Autumn hurried back across the street, where her mom was still supervising the movers. She returned in five minutes dressed in baggy gray shorts, a purple Washington Husky T-shirt, and black, low-cut, scuffed-up Adidas. No earrings. I bounce-passed her the ball, but she didn't shoot. She flipped it back to me and broke for the hoop, looking for a pass. I fed her in stride and she leaped high for a layup. She did have some hops.

For the next half-hour we worked on our shots, all over the court. Shooter and rebounder. Switch. We made a good team. If we didn't miss we got to keep shooting, so I concentrated, concentrated, concentrated.

We played twenty-one, and I took two out of three. We moved to HORSE, and she beat me three in a row. She was right-handed but could use both hands for any kind of shot: short hooks, jumpers, jump hooks, reverse layups.

I tried not to look impressed, but a question gnawed at me: How could I get that good? I was a lefty who could shoot only layups with my right. The accident had left my right arm a little stiff, a little bent, and I babied it. My right-handed attempts felt awkward, and I knew that was how they looked, too. But Autumn didn't say anything. And she used her right a lot, allowing me to shoot left. I came close all three games.

By the time we finished, we were breathing hard and sweating. Mom would have been proud.

"How about some one-on-one?" I never got workouts this good when my best friend, Lisa, came over. And she wouldn't play me one-on-one; she said I was too good for her.

"Sure."

We started. She was quick on the drive, so I gave her more space—too much. She burned me from outside. She adjusted to my left-hand drives, so I sank some jumpers. I held my own on rebounds. I could jump, too. And I knew positioning.

We were close, close, close. I beat her to fifteen, she beat me to twenty. The difference was two baskets each time.

We wilted to the grass and lay back. I smelled

trees and salt water and low tide. I could hear Autumn's breathing above the drumming of my heart.

"Nice clouds," she said.

I opened my eyes. They were nice—cottony white against the endless blue. "We learned about clouds in elementary school, but I can't remember the names of those."

"Whidbey Island clouds. In Seattle they don't look quite as fresh."

"Did you like Seattle?"

"It was my home forever. I'm still in school there."

"Which one?"

"Jefferson Middle. But it's over an hour away now, even if we hit the ferry just right."

"Two hours round trip?"

"At least. I could do homework, but I get carsick, seasick, whatever. I do best sitting at a desk."

"Not me," I said. "I go on the wildest rides at the fair and get off smiling."

"I go to the fair to eat."

Metal squawked at us from across the street. I raised up on an elbow—the scarred one. The movers had closed the doors to the truck and were following Autumn's mom into the house.

"You're almost moved in," I said, angling my elbow so the scar was more obvious. I wanted to tell Autumn about it and get that over with.

"You should see my room. Boxes and mess. It looks like my brother Noah's room."

"Is he older or younger?"

"Older. Much, he thinks. He's a sophomore at Garfield."

"Basketball player?"

"He rides the bench. But he's got those boy-muscles. I haven't beat him. Yet."

"He wouldn't ride the bench at South Whidbey High."

"That's what he thinks. We'll find out next year when we start school up here." She sat up. "You got brothers or sisters?"

"Just me." I tried to sound positive.

"And your folks."

"My dad."

"How about your mom?" She leaned toward me. "Where's she?"

I swallowed. "She died when I was five."

She stared at me. "Really?" she said. "You don't have a mom? I'm so sorry."

I shrugged, trying to make her feel better. It wasn't her fault. It was the fault of the creep who'd left Mom to die. "I don't remember her much."

"What happened?"

"A car accident." I fingered the long, ropy scar at my right elbow. Beneath it, the bone felt crooked and knobby. "It was a hit-and-run, kind of. I was with her, but I don't remember that, either."

"'Kind of' a hit-and-run?"

"A car came around a curve way too fast and crossed the center line. It didn't hit us, but it forced my mom off the road. We hit a tree head-on."

"That's where you got that?" She tipped her head at my elbow.

I nodded. "The bone was shattered. Like glass, I heard my dad say once."

"That's terrible," she said. "Does it still bother you?"

"When I let it. I'm trying not to."

"Good," she said. "Did the bad guy go to jail?"

"They never caught him. Her. Whatever." It, I wanted to say. An animal. A monster. "There was a witness, but he couldn't identify the car or the driver."

"Too bad." Autumn looked as if she wanted to ask more, but didn't. And I was ready to move on. I didn't talk much about the accident, even with Dad. I stared at the clouds again.

"Does your dad play basketball?" she said.

I felt myself smiling. "He's a chess player. An accountant. A geek, but a nice one. Mom was the athlete. She played lots of sports in high school. Basketball and track in college."

"Both?"

I nodded. "She was a guard on the basketball

team and captain of the track team at the University of Iowa."

"Wow," Autumn said. "Do you run track?"

"Four hundred and eight hundred. And the relay. My legs made it through the accident just fine. You?"

She stretched. The muscles in her calves stood out in little ridges. "Just hoops. Year-round."

"We could use you on our relay team," I said.

"You only play basketball during basketball season?" she said.

"Up here, that's the only chance we get. But basketball's my favorite sport. Once the season's over, I practice on my own."

She stood, giving me a look, drumming her fingers against her thigh.

"What?" I said.

"Thinking about possibilities." Across the street, the moving truck was lumbering away. Autumn's mom stood on the lawn and waved good-bye. "I should go help."

I stood. "Come back when you get a chance."

"Oh, I will," she said, grinning. "You've got me in your life now, girl."

## ❧ *2* ❧

# Potential to Spare

I went in and called Dad. He was in one of the meetings he used to complain about to my former sitter, Megan. Over the years, whenever he was late picking me up from her house, those meetings were his excuses. Now he thought I was old enough to be on my own after school, and Megan didn't hear the excuses as often. Now *I* got to hear about clients and partners and the IRS.

I left a message on his voice mail. "Mr. Wilde," I said, lowering my voice and trying to sound New York-ish, "this is Jane Waters, investigator with the Internal Revenue Service. It has come to my attention that you prepared and signed a tax return about which we have serious reservations. Please call me at your earliest convenience." I gave him the number for the attendance office. I was sure he wouldn't recognize it; I hadn't missed a day since entering middle school.

I called Megan. Busy signal, which meant she was on her computer, working. I decided to walk over to tell her about Autumn. But when I got outside, Autumn was hurrying across the street, ball tucked under her arm. Trying to keep up with her was a big, blocky white man in a red golf shirt and khaki shorts.

"Casey, this is my dad," Autumn announced.

He held out his hand and we shook.

"Good to meet ya, Casey." His voice was low and booming and thick with some kind of accent. The answer was embroidered on his shirt in small white letters: "Texas Longhorns." Underneath the words was the silhouette of a steer's head. "Hops tells me you're a ballplayer."

"I'm on a couple of teams, Mr. Hopkins."

"School team?"

"And a rec team. The Bruins."

"Nothing else? No select? No AAU?" He was still smiling, the smile of a bulldog.

"I've never tried out." I'd heard about select and Amateur Athletic Union teams, but this was Whidbey Island, home of art galleries and beaches and not much else. "There's none around here, and my dad's busy. I've gone to day camps."

He looked me up and down. "Five-nine or so?"

"And a half."

"Still growing, are you?"

"Mom was six-one."

"How tall's Dad?"

"Six-three." I didn't add, *Why all the questions?* I looked at Autumn for a clue, but she was focused on her dad.

"Well," he said. He looked me over again, but it didn't make me uncomfortable. I didn't feel like a girl; I felt more like something hanging on the rack at K-Mart. Not up to standards. "It's been real nice meetin' ya, Casey. I'm glad Hops has a neighbor her age."

"Me, too," I said.

"Wait, Dad." Autumn picked up my ball and tossed it to me. "Watch us for a minute. See what you think."

He stepped off the driveway and folded his arms across his broad chest. *Show me,* he seemed to be saying. "Okay."

We warmed up with a game of bump, then jumped to one-on-one. I wasn't sure what was going on, but it felt like an audition. We battled. If Autumn was trying to make me look good, she hid it well. She had a deadly outside shot, a deadly drive. And she was going at me harder than she had earlier.

But I didn't back down. I used all my skills, all my energy, and played her even. We were tied at thirteen, but she got me with left-side drives and scored the last two buckets to win, 15-13.

When I straightened up from catching my breath, Mr. Hopkins's smile was gone. He was writing something in a little notebook. He sized me up again, but this time it felt different. Not like I was from K-Mart.

"I'm a coach, Casey," he said. "Another fella and I coach Autumn's AAU team."

My heart thrummed louder. I tried to ignore it.

"The Sorcerers," Autumn said. "Fourteen-and-under."

"We've got great ballplayers from all around the Seattle area—central, south, east side, north," Mr. Hopkins said. "Our goal is to win the state championship and earn a trip to the nationals."

The nationals. I imagined where they might be. Not Langley, but New York or California. Somewhere glamorous. "I hope you do it."

"One player just moved away," Mr. Hopkins continued. "We're down to nine, and I've been keeping my eye out for talent."

I didn't dare get my hopes up. "Ten would be good."

"I like the way you play, Casey. Rough around the edges, but potential to spare. I'd like you to come to our next practice. No promises, but maybe we could use you on the Sorcerers."

"Really?" I let my heart race away.

"What's your position?"

"Post, mostly."

"On our team you'd only be semi-tall. You'll need to work on facing the hoop, driving, pulling up for the jumper. And get acquainted with that right hand. If you don't, it's like trying to swim in the ocean with one hand tied behind your back. If you're lucky, you'll stay afloat. But you're not gonna get anywhere very fast. And if you can't handle the ball with both hands, you're not gonna get very far on the basketball court. In the big time, it's sink or swim."

Sink or swim. I pictured myself drowning. But I was a good swimmer; I'd spent hundreds of hours in the pool during rehab. There was no reason I couldn't learn to use my right hand better. But could I do it fast enough for Mr. Hopkins? I wondered if he'd noticed my scar. Had Autumn told him about my arm? Was he waiting for me to use it for an excuse?

"I'll try," I said. "Where would I play?"

"Same as Hops, probably. Wing."

Wing. I was pretty sure I could play wing. But how good were these girls?

"Great," I said.

# ❧ *3* ❧

# The Anniversary

I postponed the visit to Megan's. I couldn't wait to tell Dad about Autumn and basketball, and I still had to shower and do my homework. Even with the end of the school year approaching, with our graduation party only a month away, the teachers weren't backing off.

I was upstairs in my room, figuring out some math, when I heard the garage door open. Dad was home. I hoped he'd hunted up a pizza. I was starving, and Wednesday was our traditional pizza night, which meant we both escaped cooking and dishes.

"Casey!" he called up the stairs. "You home?"

"Homeworkin'!"

"Where's my greeting?"

I went downstairs and gave him a kiss and hug. "You get pizza?"

"We'll have to scrape up something else," he said. "I was in a meeting with the IRS all afternoon." He tried to hide a smile. "An investigator named Jane Waters."

I laughed. "So did I fool you at all?" I said.

"I called the school. Then I thought I'd been given a wrong number. Until my brain went into gear. So congratulations. I owe you one, Jane."

"Where's the pizza, really?"

"Megan called. She and Dulcie are bringing homemade."

"Great!" I didn't see enough of Megan these days, or of her daughter, Dulcie, who was as much a little sister to me as I ever expected to have.

I told Dad about Autumn and her dad and basketball tryouts.

"Friday night?"

"They'll give me a ride. I don't have anything else going on. The track meet's tomorrow."

"Sounds exciting," he said. "But can you handle this and track and still maintain your grades?"

"No problem," I said. "I might not even make this team."

"All-star kids from all over?" he said. "It's an honor just getting invited."

"Yeah," I said. But my empty stomach was grumbling and tightening and creeping up into my chest.

Now I had this basketball thing, and the next day the envelope would come—maybe.

The doorbell rang. But before Dad and I could get up to answer it, I heard the door open and footsteps on the hardwood.

"Casey!" Dulcie burst into the kitchen and launched herself at me. She was eight now, but still a peanut. The only big thing about her was her voice. I caught her and held on and we exchanged a crusher bear hug.

"You're getting bigger every time I see you." She liked to hear this.

"I know," she said, squirming to the floor and standing tall. "Hi, Eith-kay." She'd discovered pig Latin when she was younger and still liked to try it out, especially on Dad.

"Ulcie-day," he said. "Where's your mom?"

"Going slow," Dulcie said.

"Maybe because I'm carrying all the stuff," Megan said as she fake-staggered into the kitchen with a grocery bag in each arm. I grabbed one, Dad grabbed the other. Like Dulcie, Megan was small. Barely five-two, barely a hundred pounds. "Little Miss Helpful," she said to Dulcie.

"I wanted to hurry," Dulcie said.

"Uh-huh." Megan moved to the counter. She unloaded pizza makings—dough, tomatoes, cheese, spices, sausage, mushrooms, peppers, onions.

She gave me a hug. She smiled up at Dad. I was hoping she'd hug him, too, but it didn't happen. It never did.

"How are you, Megan?" Dad said. I watched him watch Megan, the way I always did when she was around. But what I was looking for—a bit of shyness in his smile, a small spark deep in his eye, maybe—wasn't there.

"Good," she said. "How go your skirmishes with the IRS?"

"Funny you should ask." He gave me a grin. "I had a call today from a real hard-nosed woman."

He told her about Jane, I told her about Autumn and basketball, while we got dinner going. Dulcie helped roll the dough and ended up with streaks of flour in her dark hair and on her face. While we waited for the pizza to bake, we sat outside on the deck. We got to the subject no one had mentioned yet.

"Tomorrow's the sixteenth," I said.

"Nine years," Dad said.

"Get anything, Casey?" Megan asked. Across the table from me, Dulcie's puzzled eyes tracked from face to face.

"I checked the mail," I said. "Nothing yet."

"There's tomorrow," Dad said.

"And the next day," I said. As long as I could remember, the envelopes with my name on them and the money inside had arrived on the sixteenth—the anniversary of Mom's dying—or on the day before or the day after. No one could figure out who was sending them or why. Someone we knew, who knew her? Some rich person who'd read about her dying, who felt sorry for me? The hit-and-run driver, because he felt bad?

But would someone who'd done something so terrible even think about trying to make up for it? Not according to the sheriff's detective who'd talked to us about possibilities a few years earlier. I remembered her words: *I doubt it's blood money.* She said it was okay to talk about the money with people we trusted, but we'd already told Megan and Lisa, and that's where we stopped.

Dad didn't think it was blood money, either. Nor did Megan. Lisa and I weren't so sure. But I hoped the grownups were right. I didn't want to picture those envelopes coming from the coward who'd left Mom to die.

"You okay, Casey?" Megan looked into my eyes, searching for something. She knew me as well as she knew Dulcie, and sometimes I didn't like that. Sometimes I wanted to keep my thoughts to myself.

"I'm fine," I said, but now Dad was staring at me—his let's-see-what-we-have-in-the-fine-print look. "But," I went on, "I've been thinking that maybe we could do something more to find out what really happened. And who's sending the money. Maybe we could talk to the detective again. Or hire someone ourselves. We could use the money we get in the mail to hire a private investigator."

Dad nodded, just barely. "We could think about doing that." He sighed.

"Sometimes it's best just to let things go," Megan said. I snuck a look at Dad again, hoping to see something that still wasn't there. "Sometimes you need to put things behind you." She looked at me sadly.

"How can I?" I said. "She was my mom. And how can I forget when I get a reminder every year?"

No one looked ready to answer my question. "We'll think about it," Dad said finally. Megan got up and went inside. The oven was signaling to her.

I changed the subject. "What have you been eating, Dulcie?" She swiped crumbs from the corner of her mouth. "Cookies before you came over?"

"Mom made 'em, Asey-kay," she said. "Eanut-pay utter-bay."

I overdid it on pizza and cookies, but told myself I'd earned the extra calories with all the extra basketball. Megan and Dulcie went home and I went upstairs to do my homework.

But first I had to call Lisa.

She sounded distracted. I heard a TV in the background. She was a real addict, especially when her favorite shows were on. The hard part for me was figuring out when her favorite shows *weren't* on. It was annoying.

"I met someone new today," I said finally.

"Uh-huh."

"She moved in across the street."

"Umm."

"She's seven feet tall with stripes and purple hair."

"Really," she said as the volume of her TV rose for a commercial. Probably one of her favorites.

"Her dad's a spy, her mom's a jockey, and her brother's a pirate. With a wooden leg."

Silence. Maybe she'd slipped into a trance.

"TURN OFF THE TV!" I said.

The TV sound died. "You don't have to yell," she said. "I was listening.

"What did I say?"

More silence. "I don't have to answer that," she said finally. "You either trust me or you don't."

"I trust you," I said, "but I'll tell you again, anyway. You might want to write this down. A new girl moved in across the street. Her name's Autumn Hopkins, but everyone calls her Hops. She's nice. She's our age. She plays basketball. She's good. Her dad's a coach. He wants me to try out for his team." I told her about the team, about playing against Autumn, and about her mom and brother.

"She probably thinks you're a hick. That Langley's a hick town."

"She didn't act like that," I said.

"Won't it be embarrassing?" Lisa said.

"What?"

"Trying out? All those big-time players? If you get cut, won't you be embarrassed?"

"Who says I'm gonna get cut? If the coach didn't think I had a chance, why would he ask me to try?"

"I'd be embarrassed."

"That's because you never practice, Lisa. You spend too much time with your best friend, Mr. TV."

"You don't have to get rude. I'm just worried about your feelings."

"Then don't try to discourage me," I said.

"A new girl moves in and you forget who your friends are."

"Some friend." I hung up. But I'd gotten kind of nasty, and now I felt kind of sorry.

My phone rang. The caller ID told me it was Lisa. I didn't answer—I didn't feel *that* sorry—but downstairs Dad did. He hollered up that Lisa was on the line.

"Hi," she said, chipper. I couldn't hear her TV. "My phone went dead."

"No, it didn't," I said. "I hung up on you."

"Oh. Whatever. Sorry about what I said."

"Sorry I hung up."

"Did you get the envelope?" Lisa was one of the few people who could get over a fight in an instant and move ahead without looking back. And she almost always towed me along.

"No."

"How much do you think it'll be?"

"I don't know." Last year there'd been seventy-five hundred-dollar bills in the envelope. Dad said the first one, when I was six, contained ten hundreds. The amounts had steadily increased over the eight years, totaling $28,700. Each year he did what the instructions said: put the money into a college fund. With the earnings, there was over $40,000 now. But I would've given it up in an instant to hear Mom say my name. I would've given it up in an instant to find out who was responsible for her dying.

For my ninth birthday, Megan had given me a DVD called *The Princess Bride.* Instantly it had become my favorite movie. It was full of comedy, adventure, mystery, and romance. But it also had something else that made it special for me. One of the characters in the story, a guy named Inigo Montoya, spends the whole movie searching for the man who killed his father.

I knew how Inigo Montoya felt. The first time I watched the film, I sat there praying that he would find the black-souled killer, that he would avenge his father's death in the most satisfying way possible: a sword through the heart. The hero had only one clue:

the killer was a man with six fingers.

In movies and books the good guys almost always catch the bad guys, the ones who wrecked somebody else's life. So I couldn't understand why the real-life police had never found Mom's killer, although Dad said in real life lots of people who'd done bad things went free.

I often imagined tracking him down myself. He would have scars, or pointed ears, or fangs. Maybe one eye in the middle of his forehead. Maybe in a few years I'd be out driving my own car, looking for bad drivers, and I'd pull even with a guy weaving down the road. I'd glance over and he'd be holding a bottle in one hand. With the other, he'd be drumming out a beat on his steering wheel with his five fingers.

And a thumb. Five fingers and a thumb.

But I wasn't Inigo Montoya. And as far as anyone knew, the real-life bad guy didn't have any unusual physical trait. I didn't have a trail to follow or a clue or a sword.

I'd really only done one thing to try to find Mom's killer. After I'd finally understood what had happened to her, after I'd gotten old enough to read the newspaper, I began looking for articles on drunk drivers and hit-and-run drivers who'd been arrested. Maybe the person who'd killed Mom had been drunk another time and caused someone else to swerve off the road.

Maybe he'd hit someone and been caught.

Whenever there was a photo, I'd examine it closely to see if the face looked familiar. It never was, but I decided to do something, anyway. I cut out the articles and photos and sent them to the police-woman who'd been assigned to our case, Island County Sheriff's Detective Lainey Haller, to see if she could make some kind of connection.

She was good about sending me little thank-you notes or calling me on the phone whenever she got one of my envelopes. But nothing ever came of it. And eventually her thank-you notes and phone calls stopped. Eventually I got the hint. I quit sending the articles and photos.

Maybe it was time to talk to her again.

Lisa's TV had come back on while my mind was wandering to painful places. I didn't blame her this time. I needed a distraction, too. I decided to steer the subject away from packages of money and what that money represented. "You ready for the meet tomorrow?" I asked her.

"Ready."

We talked a while longer, and finally I got back to my homework.

It was after eleven when I went down and kissed Dad goodnight. Back upstairs, I got in bed with my lamp lit.

Next to it on my nightstand stood two pictures

of Mom. In one, she was holding me. I looked like her clone. We both had blond hair, medium length and straight. We both had blue eyes, small noses, wide smiles. We both wore jeans and yellow tops. It was the end of summer—the summer before she died—and we were brown from the sun. I was four. I must have thought she'd be with me forever.

The other picture was from Mom's college days at Iowa. In the photo she was goofing around with her 4 X 400 relay teammates. They all had their arms over each others' shoulders, they all were hamming it up: grins, one leg kicked out toward the camera, Iowa baseball caps on their heads.

I could almost feel how it must have felt to be that good, that fast, to be out in the sun with your buddies on a day when everything seemed right. I didn't like track as much as basketball, but I was good at it, and on my best days, on my team's best days, I'd had little tastes of what Mom and her friends must have experienced.

I would keep running for those little tastes. For what the future could bring. And for Mom.

I kept staring at the picture. When I looked at my clock it was after midnight. It was the anniversary of Mom's death. But as I turned out my light, I could hear her laughter. I swear I could.

# 4

## Shorts on Fire

The track meet with La Conner had dragged on. By the time the final event—the 4 X 400 meter relay—came around, the sun was closing down on the treetops, and the temperature was dropping. I'd taken a first in the 400 meter and a second in the 800 meter, where I'd let myself get too far behind early.

Lisa had chugged to third in the 400 and 800. They were good finishes for her, and I told her that, the coaches told her that, but she was wearing her long face anyway, even though she'd set personal records in both events. Track was her sport, and she didn't like finishing behind a basketball player, which was what she called me.

Dad showed up just in time for the relay. I saw him join Megan and Dulcie on the blanket they'd spread out on the grass. They'd been there since the beginning.

"Would it be okay if Lisa ran anchor just this once?" I murmured to Coach Dillard as we listened to the starter's instructions. "We're way ahead." It was true. We'd piled up points on both the boys' and girls' sides. We'd lost only three events—boys' long jump and triple jump, and girls' 1600 meter. I wanted Lisa to feel that the coaches had confidence in her.

Dillard looked at me, one eyebrow raised below her mop of red hair.

"Just this once," I repeated. "We could go back to the regular order for the district meet." I was watching Lisa, hoping she wouldn't guess what I was up to—making sure a friend got a chance to shine. She had what she called intuition, the ability to unwrap a clue before most people realized they were seeing one. And she'd never run anchor before this meet.

"You'll take her spot?" Dillard said.

"Sure. I'll go second."

"Okay," she said, and I felt myself smiling. "But get us a lead," she added.

"Don't tell anyone it was my idea," I said.

"It wasn't."

When Dillard made the announcement, I pretended to be surprised, but when the official was readying the first girls for the start, I found Lisa studying my face.

"I saw you talking to Dillard," she said.

Uh-oh. "Yeah."

"About what?"

"She asked me how I was feeling."

"What'd you say?"

"'A little tired,' I told her."

She smiled. "She must've liked the way I ran today."

"Two personal records," I said. "What's not to like?"

"Yeah." Her long face was gone.

The gun sounded. Our lead-off runner, Allison, got off to a good start, but halfway through the second curve she began to fade. Coming out of the corner, she was struggling. I could see the effort on her face. And the La Conner runner was cruising, pulling away. I'd have a lot of ground to make up.

Allison got within twenty meters of me, then fifteen. I started to jog away as the La Conner girls made their exchange. I kept reaching back, palm up, finally closing my hand around the baton. I heard Allison gasp, and I took off.

When I looked up, the second La Conner runner was already heading into the curve. I told myself to find my pace and stick with it, or I'd end up like Allison, out of gas with a hundred meters to go. I lowered my head, lengthened my stride, and settled in.

Coming out of the turn, I was gaining on the girl. Halfway up the backstretch she was maybe fifteen meters in front of me. By the time we got to the second turn I was within ten and feeling strong. I saw her glance back. I surged, and hung on her outside shoulder, gathering my strength, waiting for her kick. But she didn't have a kick. I blew past her.

I passed the baton to Katie, our third girl, with a fifteen-meter lead. "Great job," Dillard told me. Lisa put her arm around my waist and said, "Thanks for the lead."

The third La Conner runner wasn't giving up. By the time Katie was fifty meters from the finish line, she was ahead by only ten. Lisa stepped out on the track. Next to her was the girl who'd beaten her in the 400. "Run like your shorts are on fire," I told Lisa, and she grinned. She started off, jogging. Katie caught her for a good exchange, but Lisa was only six or seven meters ahead going into the curve.

The La Conner girl ran smart, shadowing Lisa through the turn. But Lisa was a smoothie—head steady, arms loose. Halfway up the straight, she still had a five-meter lead.

It shrank through the curve. The La Conner runner was tall and determined, and she had Lisa in her sights, just a meter or two behind entering the home straight. But Lisa's jaw slid out, the way it did when she was psyching herself up for a fight. I found myself jumping up and down. So were Allison and Katie. So was Dillard. The crowd was on its feet.

They looked even at fifty meters, at forty, at thirty, but then suddenly Lisa dug deeper, suddenly she had a one-meter lead. "All the way through!" I screamed, and she did it. She sprinted all the way through the finish line, holding on to that slim margin, chesting through the tape first.

We let her shake hands with the La Conner girl and get the first-place confirmation from the official, then we jumped her. Her smile was wide, even as she collapsed to the grass as the rest of us piled on and Dillard stood over us, grinning. I thought of the photo of Mom and her track pals. My teammates and I weren't all grown-up, not yet, but this felt like more than a taste. How much better could anything feel than what I was feeling just now?

"You ran like the wind," Allison said.

"Like my shorts were on fire," Lisa said. We all laughed.

# ❧ 5 ❧

# Blood Money

Dad barely had the Jeep in the garage when I jumped out and headed for the mailbox.

It was filled with the usual stuff—bills and junk. I went through the stack twice, like some little kid hoping for a party invitation.

"Not there?" Dad said.

"There's still tomorrow."

"One of these years it could end," he said.

"You say that every year."

"It's true every year."

"You don't have to baby me," I said. "I'm not going to be depressed if the money stops. Part of me feels excited to get it, but the other part feels sick. When the physical therapist used to make me stretch and stretch my arm to make it better, I would almost throw up. This feels kind of like that."

"You were a trouper then," Dad said. "You're a trouper now." He put a long thin arm around my shoulders. He pulled me close and I snuggled in.

We'd gotten take-out burgers and fries on the way home. I downed mine and left Dad finishing his at the kitchen table. I needed to think about something else. Outside, the sun had dropped below a bank of pink night clouds, leaving me with perfect practice conditions—cooling, a light breeze, no rain, no sun in my eyes but still plenty of light.

I started in close—right side, left side, right hand, left hand—and worked my way out to the free throw line. I shot fifty, sinking forty-two. Thirty-seven were clean. I was working my way around the three-point circle when I heard a voice.

"Who says you don't see girls out shootin' hoops?" I turned. It was Mr. Hopkins. Next to him stood his wife. Next to her was Autumn.

"Mr. Hopkins," I said. "I've never heard anybody say that."

"I hear it all the time. It's what the guys who've never watched women's basketball say. 'The reason girls aren't any good is because they're not dedicated. Basketball's just a social thing. You never see 'em working on their game on their own.'"

The words got under my skin. "They need to drive through this neighborhood."

"Or past the city playgrounds," Autumn said.

"They'll see girls takin' it to the guys, not backin' down."

Mr. Hopkins smiled. "Casey, this is Autumn's mom. The source of Autumn's looks and talent."

"And brains," Mrs. Hopkins said. She laughed a nice laugh and held out her hand.

"Hi," I said, shaking her hand. "I'm glad you've moved here."

"Me, too, Casey." She looked around and breathed deep. "I've wanted to move out of the city for a long time. This seems like a little corner of God's country."

The front door opened. Dad came out and met everyone. Mr. Hopkins worked in Mukilteo, just a ferry ride away, for a software company. Mrs. Hopkins was a graphic designer who worked mostly out of their home. Megan and Dulcie walked down from their house, and there were more introductions.

"You like to shoot hoops, pretty girl?" Autumn asked Dulcie.

She nodded. We let her shoot while Autumn and I rebounded. Dulcie concentrated on every shot, eyes narrowed, tongue peeking from the corner of her mouth.

I looked up the street and spotted Lisa a half-block away. Starting toward us. Hesitating. I waved. Now she couldn't pretend she didn't see me and the others. She'd have to keep coming.

I waited for her until she arrived, but Autumn beat me to an introduction. "I'm Autumn," she said to Lisa. "The new neighbor."

Lisa worked up a smile. "Hi," she said, not volunteering her name.

"This is Lisa," I said. "My friend." I introduced her to Autumn's folks. She was polite but tongue-tied. I couldn't tell if she was shy or jealous or both, but now that I'd admitted she was my friend, I hoped she'd act a little more normal.

The adults kept talking; Dulcie and Autumn kept shooting. I only watched, afraid Lisa would feel left out if I joined in. She stood next to me, arms folded, silent.

"Wanna go over to my house for a while?" she asked me finally.

I didn't have an answer right off, and she probably took that as my answer because she sighed and began moving away. But I had to say something. "Maybe later. I don't want to leave with everyone still here."

"Everyone?" she said.

"You know what I mean. It would be rude."

"Yeah," she said. "Your best friend is less important than your...neighbor." She slipped away while I fought down the urge to not let her have the last word. As I watched her head toward home, I wondered how I was going to get the Lisa part of my life together with the new part of my life. Lisa didn't like new.

I went back to basketball, rebounding Dulcie's shots, seeing how high I could peak when I grabbed the ball, seeing how fast I could pass it to Autumn.

When I next looked at the adults, there was another body there. Thin, dark wavy hair, taller than Mr. Hopkins but shorter than Dad. "Is that your brother, Autumn?"

"Himself. Wants money or the car keys." She shook her head. "Come here, girlfriends," she said, and started toward her brother. Dulcie beamed.

Autumn waited while her brother shook hands with Megan and Dad. "Hey, Noah," she said finally. "Say hello to Casey and Dulcie."

I expected he'd feel put-upon, but he smiled and said he was glad to meet us. Then he left with his dad's car keys. Dulcie watched him go, still beaming. An instant Noah groupie.

"It's okay if Casey goes to the big city with us tomorrow?" Mr. Hopkins asked Dad.

"She's looking forward to it," Dad said. "She's assured me she can handle this and everything else."

"No doubt," Mr. Hopkins said. "I've seen that old determination thing in her eyes."

Dulcie looked up at my face, as if she really expected to see something there. And maybe she did. But if she saw determination, she probably also saw a little nervousness, a little reluctance, a little lack of confidence. But none of that was going to keep me from giving it a try. None of it.

Lisa seemed standoffish the next day. I didn't see her in the halls, and she didn't sit with me at lunch. I decided to break the ice.

I flopped onto the bus seat next to her after track practice. "I'm sorry you got upset last night," I said over the noise of the engine and the wind through the windows and the jumble of voices. Dust specks swirled in the air and danced up my nose. I sneezed, loud. Some comedian boys sitting around us started fake-sneezing.

"Upset? I wasn't exactly upset." Her jaw came out and her eyes narrowed. Ready for round one. "But you could've come to my house."

"Autumn's been friendly to me," I said. "She's my across-the-street neighbor. Her parents are nice. Her dad's giving me a tryout. The least I can do is be nice to her. I couldn't just leave."

Lisa looked straight ahead, unblinking, while I waited for some kind of reply. What I'd just told her—that I was being nice to Autumn because she and her family had been nice to me—wasn't the whole truth. I *wanted* Autumn for a friend. And maybe Lisa's intuition told her that.

"You'll always be my best friend," I told her.

She smiled a little. She turned toward me, finally.

"You want to come over now?" I said. "I'm gonna check the mail." Knowing that Lisa understood what I was waiting for made me feel like I wasn't alone. It was a good feeling.

"What if it's not there?" she said

I shrugged, forcing a smile.

"I'll come," she said. "Just in case it's not."

We got off at my stop and raced for the mailbox. I rubbed my elbow for luck while Lisa stared at the little door.

"Go ahead," I said.

She didn't have to be asked twice. She flipped down the door and we peered inside.

Empty.

Then I heard the sound of an engine. From up the street the mail truck was heading our way, running a little late.

It pulled up to the curb next to our mailbox. "Girls," the mailman said, fishing around inside the truck.

He handed me the mail through his open door. I didn't dare look, but there was a stack of stuff.

The mailman drove off. I handed Lisa the mail. She sorted through it. Junk. Bill. Junk.

Brown envelope, my name, no return address, padded, fat.

I glanced up and down our tree-lined street. Quiet. No one in sight besides the mail truck. No one to swoop down and swipe the package.

"Is it okay if you open it?" Lisa said.

"Inside, my dad said."

"Let's go." She started for my front door.

"Wait. Let's take it to Megan's."

Lisa nodded, although I could see her excitement wilt. She wasn't much for sharing with anyone, even Megan.

We hurried to Megan's house. She let us in, eyeing the envelope. "Is that it?" she said, as we headed to her kitchen.

"We just got it," I said. "We thought you'd like to be in on the opening."

"Thanks," Megan said. "But let's make it quick. Dulcie's due home from a friend's, and I'm not sure I could explain this to her."

Lisa lay the envelope on the table and carefully unzipped it. Inside was a typed note. She handed it to me, but I'd already read it over her shoulder. The wording was the same as always: "For your college, Casey. Be someone special."

Lisa pulled out a bundle wrapped in brown paper. It was the size of folding money. She tore it open, not so carefully.

Ben Franklins. Hundred-dollar bills. Lots of them. She gave some to me, some to Megan, kept some. We counted, then added. One hundred hundred-dollar bills. Ten thousand dollars.

"Wow!" Lisa said.

"The most I've ever gotten." My voice sounded funny, even to me. I was in the grip of a half-excited, half-empty feeling. Part of me wanted to recount the money, to feel that fat stack of cash in my hands. Part of me wanted to give it to Dad and never see it again.

I wrapped up the money and stuck it back in the envelope. Under the glare of the kitchen light, I could make out the postmark. It was the same as always: San Francisco. A big city where we didn't know anyone. So who in San Francisco knew us? Or me, at least? Or felt sorry for me? Or guilty? The postmark was our only clue, but the postmarks hadn't helped us or the Sheriff's Department. According to Dad, Lainey Haller had tried tracing the envelopes. For the first few years she'd even had the envelopes and money checked for fingerprints. Nothing useful had shown up, and now no one even checked. They'd given up, but I hadn't. I still read newspapers and watched the news on TV, looking for a familiar face.

As I stowed the envelope in my backpack, I thought about a six-fingered man and a sword to the heart.

"Careful with that on the way home," Megan said. She smiled, but her eyes looked sad.

## ❦ *6* ❦

# Bright Lights, Big Tryout

Practice was at Autumn's school, Jefferson Middle, in Seattle. I looked forward to the trip with Autumn and her dad. Seattle was like a different world from our quiet island, and I didn't get there much.

We caught the ferry from the south end of Whidbey. As the big boat pulled away, I stood on the deck and looked back across the churning water at the little ferry-dock town of Clinton, the beach houses, the sun hanging above thick evergreen forests. Somewhere back there, five miles or so up the road, through trees, past meadows, was Langley, where I'd spent almost my whole life.

Now I was getting a chance to experience something else. I knew it would be different. I hoped it would last longer than one night.

We docked at Mukilteo, then headed to the freeway and south into the big city. Traffic was thick and slow, but Mr. Hopkins seemed used to it. He talked basketball as he weaved in and out of the other cars, which were all driven by what he called Sunday drivers, and turned his country music up and down according to the conversation.

Me, I'd tried to look nice: double ponytail, a little mascara, new Carolina-blue shirt and shorts, mid-high white Jordan retros with blue laces. I left my earrings on my dresser—coaches and refs frowned on earrings—but I tried to make up for it with a double layer of lip gloss and a smidgen of blush.

We parked. I half-wanted to stay sitting in the back of Mr. Hopkins's cozy Outback and wait for practice to be over, to forget the whole tryout thing. But I grabbed my bag and followed Autumn and her dad out of the car.

"So what do you think?" Autumn said.

"Awesome," I said, and it was, in a way. Langley Middle School was old, but Jefferson looked ancient. It was awesome to think about how long ago it had been built, and how many kids had gone through it. And that it was still standing.

We were early, so Autumn decided to show me around. I saw one of her classrooms, the girls' bathroom, a science lab that smelled worse than the bathroom. On the way to the gym we passed the library. The door was wide open and a light was on, so I walked in and looked around.

I was surprised. At Langley Middle School we had a separate library building that was a magnet for kids. You walked through weathered double doors and up worn wooden stairs and all of a sudden you were in this big, two-level room with high ceilings that was like an old-movie version of a giant study in a country mansion.

Once, a long time before, the space had been the school's theater. Now the old stage was a comfy loft complete with easy chairs, and at the other end of the room sat cushy couches. Soft music played, computers hummed, magazines and newspapers and paperbacks were within easy reach. And wherever there was room, there were bookcases jammed with books.

Sometimes, especially on rainy days, I'd go in there at lunchtime and sit at a table or on a big overstuffed couch and do my homework, kind of. Mostly I'd just gaze through the windows at the fields and woods or look around the shelves at all the journeys waiting to be taken. I'd just breathe in the smell.

The library at Jefferson was a different story. There were tables and chairs and computers. And bookshelves, lots of them. But they were mostly empty, and the lonely books looked old and beaten-up. On a few half-empty racks were some dog-eared magazines. I breathed in. This library even smelled different.

"The school doesn't get much money for books and stuff," Autumn said from the doorway. She looked apologetic. I wondered if she'd seen something on my face.

"It's not that bad," I said. "But I think you'd like Langley's."

"Let's go," she said. We left, with me wondering how there could be such a difference. It wasn't fair that some schools had more money than others.

But I had something else to think about— basketball. Walking down a shadowy hallway, I checked my shirtsleeve. It was long enough to cover most of my scar for now, but not once the action started. I tried to think of clever answers to a familiar question: what happened to your arm? I couldn't think of any; I never had. I'd have to rely on the truth, painful as it was.

We pushed through some doors. The gym was an improvement over the library. It had modern baskets and backboards—lots of them—and bright lights and a nice wooden floor. And it was big.

We were early, but one girl was already there. She was at the far end, stretching, and as we dropped our bags and sat, she got down in a pushup position and started pumping them off. She hadn't noticed us, so I knew she wasn't trying to impress anyone. This was a *serious* team.

While we were putting on our shoes, the girl saw us and came over. She was about my height.

"This is Casey," Autumn said. "This is Vanessa." We nodded. Autumn and Vanessa looked like they could be sisters, although Vanessa was a bit darker and thin enough to be a model. "Casey's gonna be trying out," Autumn said.

"Good to meet you," I said.

"Yeah." She smiled, but it was one of those smiling-to-yourself kinds of smiles. Cute but cool. "Coach told us he was looking for another body."

"Uh-uh," Autumn said. "Casey's a player."

"Oh?" Vanessa looked me up and down. "What's your position?"

"Maybe wing, Mr. Hopkins says. He says you have a couple of post players already."

"We've got a couple wings, too." She wagged her finger between herself and Autumn.

"There's always the bench," I said, trying to be funny and humble.

"Yeah," she said again. Autumn gave her a look, but Vanessa just walked away.

Welcome to the big time, I thought.

"Don't mind her," Autumn said. "She only just

became a starter. She's what you might call insecure. But she'll come around."

We went to a basket and shot and rebounded while more players showed up. Autumn introduced me to them. Unlike Vanessa, they were all friendly. Sara from Bellevue, Carley from Renton, Thea from Kent, Rachel from Edmonds, Cristina from Woodinville. The last two girls to arrive—DJ and Ashley—were from Seattle. They were both blond, both over six feet. I felt like a little kid shaking hands with them. DJ was wider, with big shoulders. Ashley looked like a runner.

"Vanessa's from Seattle, too," Autumn said when we were back by ourselves. "So there's four from the city, five from the 'burbs, and one from the sticks."

"Two, now."

Hops grinned. "I'll have to get used to that."

A whistle blasted. We ran to the center of the court, where Mr. Hopkins and another man stood. No one said a word. This *was* a serious team.

"You met everyone, Casey?" Mr. Hopkins said.

I told him yes and he introduced me to Carley's dad, Jimmy Young, the assistant coach. He was tall—six-four, maybe.

"Casey's here to take a look at us," Mr. Hopkins said, "and we're gonna take a look at her. For this audition to work, you need to share the ball with her in all the drills and scrimmages." I felt my face getting hot. "In other words, treat her like a teammate."

"Amen," Jimmy said. His brown head was shaved bald, and little beads of sweat had formed in the wrinkles of his scalp. The gym was warm.

We got in a tight circle and yelled "Sorcerers!" then broke to the baseline for drills. We started with controlled dribbling with a defender. I partnered with Autumn and did okay. I didn't fall on my rear or dribble the ball off my foot. From there we went to chest passes up and down the court, three-man weave, fast break drill, three-on-two, two-on-one transition drill, half-court weave with layups, and more. I began to feel comfortable. I knew the drills from camps and my own teams' practices.

I looked around at what the other players were doing. And the nerves returned. Because they were good. Rachel and Cristina, who were both five-five or five-six, were quick and slick magicians. Point guards, obviously. But *everyone* could handle the ball. With both hands. I fingered my scar, my ready-made excuse. We ran lines, and DJ, the biggest girl on the team, finished second to Autumn. I wasn't last, at least. Maybe fifth. No worse than sixth.

We took a water break. Finally! Then we were back at it. We went to a two-line relay race. I was second in our line behind Vanessa. Going down I did great. We had the lead. But coming back my dribble got away from me. Then I missed my shot. By the time I finally made it, we were fifty feet behind.

I slunk back to the end of my line, where I got to face Vanessa. She frowned. "Where'd you learn to dribble?"

"I can dribble." I studied my right elbow. I imagined her noticing the scar, saying, *Oh, you had a bad injury? You dribble and shoot real good, considering.*

"Coulda fooled me," she said. "You cost us the lead."

"What do you get if you win?" We were still a half-court back with one person to go.

"You get to hold your head up," she said.

But we lost.

We moved on to an around-the-world competition, where I couldn't hit anything, and then to free throws, where I canned nine of ten and got smiles from Thea and Jimmy. He talked a lot, encouraging us, but Mr. Hopkins didn't say much. He took notes. Whenever I screwed up, I'd look at him and he'd be taking notes. Sometimes he was looking at me and talking to Jimmy.

Another break. I got a drink, then leaned against the wall, catching my breath, looking around the old gym. Over in the far corner, Autumn and Vanessa were having a head-to-head conversation. They peeked in my direction. They were talking about me.

With a half-hour left, Jimmy split up the team for a scrimmage. I felt the little knot in my stomach swell up and tighten. My last chance to show my stuff.

The teams were the same as we had for the relay and around-the-world, so it was Rachel, Ashley, Thea, Vanessa, and me versus Autumn and her crew.

I had a few low points—mishandling a perfect pass from Rachel on the break and letting it trickle out of bounds, having DJ cram a shot down my throat. Hearing Vanessa laugh.

But a minute later she was giving Carley a bad time over a wayward pass. It felt good to have some company. And I shot pretty well from outside—two for four on three-pointers—and I scored on drives. I did okay at wing, although I had a hard time when the coaches slowed us down to run the offense. I did better when everyone was flying up and down the court. I played okay defense on Autumn. She got no easy points.

The score seemed even. I wasn't hurting my team.

We cooled down with free throws sandwiched between more sets of lines. I'd just sunk four in a row when Mr. Hopkins called me to the sideline. I'd seen him and Jimmy talking, but now he was alone, flipping through his little notebook. My heart stalled.

"I liked your effort tonight, Casey," he said.

"Thanks, Mr. Hopkins."

"Knowledge and skills are important," he said, "but effort can make up for deficiencies. I liked the way you worked. You didn't back down."

I could sense a *but* coming. I held my breath.

"I did see some shortcomings, though."

I nodded, willing to admit to them, as long as he let me on the team.

"Mostly, inexperience at the wing position, and no experience with our offensive and defensive sets."

"Uh-huh." I swallowed.

"You can learn that stuff at practices," he said. "But you'll have to do some work on your own. You need to be able to use that right hand to dribble-drive, shoot, and pass. As naturally as you use your left. Without thinking."

He stared at me, while my stomach churned. "One hand might do for a swimming pool, but you're gonna be out in the big waves, trying to keep your head above water, trying to make headway."

"I am, Mr. Hopkins?"

He smiled. "And call me Duncan. Or Coach." He tipped back his baseball cap. "Welcome to the Sorcerers."

I took a deep breath, finally. The gym had grown quiet. "Thanks!" I said. "Thanks, Coach!" I turned. The team—the rest of *my* team—was gathered around the center circle with Jimmy. They clapped, loud and long. All of them.

# ❧ *7* ❧

# Stranger in Town

**S**aturday I hurried over to Megan's. I couldn't wait to tell her my good news. When I got to her driveway, a strange car sat in front of her garage.

I continued on down the street toward Lisa's house, then circled back. The car—a white Toyota—was still there.

Megan's door opened. I heard voices. A young man, tall and blond, stepped out, followed by Megan and Dulcie. Feeling like an intruder, I backed into the shadows of some bushes.

"It was great seeing you, Megan," the guy said. "You look good."

I got this empty feeling in my chest. I peered through the shrubs. Megan really didn't look so good. Her hair was a work-in-progress. She wasn't wearing makeup. She wore khaki shorts and her

Lyle Lovett T-shirt. She was barefoot. So why was he saying she looked good? Was he *in love* or something?

"Thanks." I thought—hoped—she sounded kind of halfhearted.

The guy crouched, eye-level with Dulcie. He stuck out his hand. "It was wonderful meeting you, Dulcie."

She took it and he held on. "Thanks, Mr.—"

"Call me Rex." He stood. "You're going to be a beauty."

He let go of her hand, finally, then leaned over and kissed Megan. He was going for her lips, but she half-turned her head and he ended up getting her on the cheek. No problem. He smiled and went to his car.

"I'll call you," he said.

I quit looking. I ducked down to where the bushes thickened. His engine started, he backed out. I watched as the shiny-white rolled past my hiding place.

The car accelerated down the street. I stayed put, wondering. Did Megan have a boyfriend? Had she gotten tired of waiting around for Dad—if she'd *ever* been waiting around for Dad?

I stalled five minutes and went to her door. I pretended to be winded, as if I'd just run from my house. Dulcie opened the door and dragged me to the kitchen, where Megan was making coffee, her back to me. When she turned, she wore that phony mouth-only smile.

"Can I get you something, Case?" she said. "Cereal?"

"Not hungry." My stomach was full of something, but not food. It felt like a wasp's nest, buzzing and prickly.

She sat with me at the table. "So, what's up?" she said, searching my eyes.

I'd almost forgotten why I'd come. "Guess." But my face must have given me away.

"You made the team." Now she gave me a real smile.

I nodded, and she hugged me, long and tight. Dulcie jumped around the kitchen, both arms raised. Megan poured us orange juice and made a toast. "To Casey. Someday we'll see her on TV." We sat quietly for a minute while I enjoyed the celebration and thought about playing in front of TV cameras.

"Are you working today?" I said.

"Maybe later," Megan said. "Dulcie's trying to talk me into a trip to Deception Pass. You wanna come?"

"I don't know," I said, thinking about Duncan's words: *Sink or swim.* "My game needs work."

Megan gave me a distracted nod.

"I thought I saw a car pulling out of your driveway earlier," I said. "I thought it might be someone delivering work." I knew the realtors and banks Megan worked for didn't usually deliver their mortgage papers to her, but I was fishing.

She took her time answering. "Loan and title stuff. Not due until next week."

How could she be telling the truth? What about that kiss? If she had a boyfriend, wouldn't she tell me? I wanted to ask more, but I decided I'd pushed it far enough. Maybe if I went to the beach, Megan would talk more about her visitor. And if I went, Mr. Mystery probably wouldn't. "What time are you going?"

"About eleven," Megan said. "Can you take the time off?"

"Sure," I said. "I'll practice basketball after we get back."

Dulcie squeezed my hand. "Minus tide at noon!" she said. "Tide pools! Sea stars and hermit crabs and eels!"

"And a giant octopus to give you a hug," I said.

"Like this!" Dulcie leaped up, arms around my neck, legs around my waist. She was light but wiry, and it took me a while to peel her off. Megan smiled, but her eyes had a far-off, worried look.

I took a break from my detective work on the drive up the island. But after we arrived at the park, while Megan and I watched Dulcie explore tide pools and dig in the sand, I tried to find out more about Rex.

I couldn't just let this go. I'd never known Megan to go out with anyone, but I'd always pictured her and Dad together. As far as I knew, they'd never been more than friends, but how could they get to be more than friends if she began seeing someone else? "Does Dulcie ever miss having a dad?" I said.

Megan gave me a quick look and then turned away. "One who's actually around, you mean?" she said finally. And she was right. Dulcie had a dad somewhere. Back east, Megan said. Out of the picture.

"Yeah," I said. "One who's around."

"Not that I've noticed," she said. "She's never known her dad. So can she miss him?"

"Not him, maybe," I said. "But just having a dad. I didn't know my mom much, but I miss having a mom." With me, it felt like I'd been robbed of a piece of my heart. I didn't know what that piece did, exactly, but I could feel the emptiness deep inside, where it had been.

"She's got me," Megan said. "She's got you. And your dad's been great to her."

"But do you ever think about meeting someone who could be more like a dad to her? Someone you'd think about marrying?"

"There are worse things than not having a dad," Megan said. "Like having the wrong dad. Or a stepdad from hell. I'm pretty happy the way things are. And I think Dulcie is, too." Megan faced me. "Look at her."

I did. Dulcie was skipping rocks now, carefree. I couldn't argue about her being happy. And I felt happier myself. I still didn't know anything about Megan's visitor, but it didn't sound like she was getting ready to jump into a relationship with both feet. One toe at a time, maybe?

It was nearly four when we got home. Megan had errands to run, and I told her I'd keep an eye on Dulcie, who was willing to be my rebounder. She was in a good mood. We'd had a picnic lunch and explored more tide pools and collected shells and rocks. But for much of the afternoon I worried about not practicing basketball. I kept thinking about my new teammates, how good they were. They didn't get that way by digging in the sand. I thought about my not-so-great right hand.

There was a question I'd never asked Dad. I started for the house, Dulcie trailing. "How about some lemonade and cookies?" I said to her.

She beat me to the front door. I left her in the kitchen with a stack of chocolate-chip cookies, a tall glass of lemonade, a *Captain Underpants*, and directions to stay put.

Dad looked up when I walked into his office.

"What hand did I use before the accident?"

I said. We always said "the accident." It was like a password that opened a semisecret file. We didn't discuss "the accident" much, and if I'd asked the question before, I didn't remember the answer.

Dad stared at me.

"Was I left-handed before my arm got smashed, before the surgeries?"

"No," he said. "But you were in casts for most of a year. You adjusted."

"Adjusted?" Was it too long ago to remember, or had I just shoved the memory to a dark, secret spot in my head?

"It took you a while," he said. "At the time of the accident, you were right-handed. But once your right arm was out of commission, you worked at figuring out how to use that left hand like no five-year-old has worked at anything. The doctor looked at your tenacity and predicted you'd be able to accomplish anything you ever set your heart on. And you were proud of yourself, what you could do as a one-handed southpaw. By the time the cast finally came off, you'd learned how to eat, write, comb your hair, brush your teeth, throw a ball, shoot a basket—all left-handed. You mostly didn't go back."

I remembered some of it—the hospital, the trips to Doctor Ostrom's office, the clunky casts, the sling around my neck, sitting while other kids were playing, gritting my teeth against the pain. Or maybe what I remembered mostly was the stories, what Dad or Megan had told me—except the pain. That memory lived in my bones. "So I used to be okay with my right hand?"

He turned a picture frame on his desk so I could see it. It was my art—a crayoned figure of Dad standing under what seemed to be an apple tree. A bright sun with rays spread across a purple sky. "You gave me this on Father's Day," Dad said. "The year before the accident. You drew it right-handed. You did everything right-handed before the accident."

So my right hand wasn't some rookie that needed to be taught *everything* from scratch. It just needed to remember how good it used to be. I decided to give it a cram course. I decided I would start running to school with my basketball, dribbling it all the way. Right-handed.

Dulcie and I went back out. I shot right-handed, telling myself it felt perfectly natural.

"Hey, Casey! Hey, Dulcie!" Autumn was in her driveway, waving her arms. "Come here, girlfriends!"

Dulcie scurried toward her new friend. I followed.

"Come around back," Autumn said when we reached her yard. The last time I'd seen her, her hair had been kind of straight down. Now it was in small braids all over. It looked cool.

We walked around the side. I stopped, staring. A small bulldozer sat in the middle of the lawn. Men were staking out a big rectangular area, measuring and pounding and stringing. Autumn's mom and dad and brother stood nearby, arms crossed under their chests like they were a supervision team.

"The girls!" Duncan yelled. Dulcie and I waved and moved closer. Noah nodded in our general direction. At least I imagined he did. Sometimes you had to give a boy the benefit of the doubt.

"What is it?" I said.

"A swimming pool," Dulcie guessed, and for a second I thought she was right. Then I knew.

"You're having a court put in?" I couldn't believe it. I'd bugged Dad about a court, but he'd looked at prices and told me it would be cheaper to send me to camps for ten years. And he wouldn't have to give up his backyard pond and gardens.

"What do you think?" Autumn said. "It's kinda like a reward—or bribery, maybe—for me and Noah having to switch schools."

"Awesome," I said, but that wasn't a strong enough word.

"I wanna switch schools," Dulcie said.

Autumn laughed. "Plenty of room for everyone here. You guys are welcome whenever, even if we're not around."

"Really?" I said. "Could Lisa use it, too? She's on my other teams."

"Anyone," Autumn said. "Is she good?"

"She tries," I said. "Track's her sport."

We went out front. Dad was in our yard with Megan. "Come here!" I called, waving. My right arm felt heavy. I wasn't used to using it as much as I had in the past few days.

"We wanna show you something!" Dulcie yelled.

They waved back and crossed the street. They looked good together—tall and angular, small and curvy. I pictured them holding hands and thought about Megan's visitor. Why *didn't* Dad make a move? I appreciated his loyalty to Mom, but nine years was way beyond extreme.

Autumn showed them the site for the court and described the plans. They talked with Autumn's folks a while, then left, taking Dulcie with them, leaving Autumn and me.

"Are your dad and Megan going out?" Autumn said.

"She's watched me since Mom died. She's like a favorite aunt, Dulcie's like a kid sister, but Megan and Dad..." I didn't know what to say about their non-relationship.

"She's from here?"

"She grew up in her house. She inherited it when her mom died."

61

"Where's Dulcie's daddy?"

"Back east somewhere. He never calls or sees her."

"They weren't married?"

I shook my head.

"Megan seems kind of happy-sad."

"I think so, too," I said. "Just lately."

"Maybe 'cause your dad won't ask her out."

I laughed. "Megan's not shy. She could ask."

"Some folks are just slow. It could still happen."

"I thought so, too. Until this morning." I told Autumn about the guy, the kiss. I felt a little like a traitor, like if I was going to talk about this, it should be with Lisa. But Lisa wasn't around, and Autumn was asking.

"She turned her face away?" Autumn said.

I nodded.

"Good sign," Autumn said. Now there were two of us who thought so.

"Can I ask you something?" I said.

She gave me a little grin. "Sounds serious."

I shrugged. "I hope not."

"Ask."

"At practice last night, I saw you and Vanessa talking and kind of looking at me."

Autumn kept her grin going. "Yeah?"

"Were you talking about me?"

"Sort of. But it was mostly about her, and I did

most of the talking. She was worried about losing her starting position. I told her not to take it out on you. I told her my dad and Jimmy would play the girls who work hard and support their teammates."

"That was it?"

"I told her you were going to be a teammate, and she better get used to it."

"You said that—you knew it—even before your dad and Jimmy decided?"

"Casey girl, I knew it from the first time I saw you shooting hoops in your driveway."

That night I called Lisa right after dinner. We talked almost every night, and sometimes I didn't have a lot to say. But now I did. I told her about my day, about what I'd seen at Megan's, about the beach.

I didn't tell Lisa that she wasn't the first person I'd told about the mystery man. She would have been hurt. But I still wanted to talk, and talking to Lisa was comfortable.

With Lisa, I didn't have to explain a lot. Lisa knew how much I wanted Dad and Megan to get together, and she seemed interested and sympathetic and friendly until I mentioned Autumn and her new court. "She wants you to see it."

"Whatever."

*Whatever?* Why wouldn't Lisa give Autumn and her family a chance? They were great! Would I be jealous if a new girl moved in across the street from Lisa and suddenly started attracting Lisa's attention? I told myself that I was more grown-up. "I won't be riding the bus for a while," I said, to change the subject.

"Why not?"

"I'm gonna run back and forth to school. Dribbling. I need to work my right hand."

"Why's that?"

"Coach says so. I made the team."

For a moment there was silence on her end. "That's great," she said finally, sounding as if she meant it. "I knew you could do it the whole time."

"Thanks," I said.

"I could help you," she said. "With basketball. Working on your right hand."

"Really?"

"Sure. I know I'm not exactly an all-star, but I could give you someone to practice your stuff on. I could be like the stand-in for a real basketball player whenever you don't have one around."

"You can play ball, Lisa."

"I'm a runner. I know that. But I'll give it a try."

I was quiet a minute. I knew Lisa didn't love basketball. "I won't forget your offer," I said. "Thanks."

She really *was* a good friend—my best friend. But did that mean I couldn't have another friend, too?

## ❧ *8* ❧

# Creeps

Monday's run to school—nearly two miles of neighborhood streets and back roads—had gone okay. The weather was cloudy and cool, and I worked up only a thin layer of sweat.

I was on my way home after track practice, a half-mile or so to go, when I caught the deep-base, ground-quaking rumble of speakers behind me. Headlights blinked in the early-evening gloom. I moved farther onto the shoulder, expecting the car to pass.

It didn't. It pulled even with me, moving at jogging speed. Out of the corner of my eye I saw a shape—red, shiny, low. Unfamiliar. I tucked my ball under my arm. I kept running.

The front of the car inched ahead of me. I was on a section of road with no houses. No one could see me. I put my head down and tried to breathe. The bass grew louder.

"Hey, stretch!" A man's voice. I kept my head down. I looked at the up-and-down of my bare legs and wished I'd worn sweats, not shorts.

"Hey, superstar!" A different voice, deeper, slipping under my skin and sending graveyard-willies up my spine.

I kept my pace. I kept my eyes straight ahead, willing them not to tear up. *Don't stop*, I told myself. *Don't talk.*

"Need a ride somewhere, sweetheart?" The first voice, creepy-friendly.

I looked at the woods that bordered the road, thought for a second about taking off into them. But I didn't want to be alone in the woods.

"Thirsty, baby?" The deep voice again. I sensed the car edging closer, onto the shoulder. I glanced over. The driver—twenty, maybe, long dark hair, ragged goatee—held up a silver can. "You look hot." Next to him a guy who might have been his brother leaned from the open window, way too close, with a gash of a smile on his thin, pale face.

I got my eyes back on my path. I sped up, my stomach in my throat. Maybe I should turn around and sprint the other way. But home was ahead of me, less than a half-mile now. I thought about the ten weeks of karate I'd taken when I was in sixth grade.

Did I remember any of it? Did it matter? I'd try to fight them if I had to, but I'd only make them mad. I'd lose.

*Go away,* I thought. *Go back to your hole.*

Suddenly a white car whipped around the red car and swerved in front of it. The white car slowed, then stopped. The red car braked behind it, whisper-close, and I raced past both of them.

Behind me the bass slowly died. An engine roared. Tires shrieked.

The road curved. Houses appeared. Without slowing, I looked back. The red car was smoking through a U-turn.

I stopped. My heart galloped. My breathing came from some achy place deep in my lungs.

The driver of the white car was out, staring after the red car. He got back in and closed the door. His car started toward me. Should I run?

Something told me no. I wasn't sure my legs would work, anyway.

The car stopped next to me. The passenger-side window hummed down.

It was Megan's visitor from the other day. Rex.

"You all right?" he said.

I nodded.

"You looked like you didn't want to talk to those guys."

"No." My voice sounded funny. Tight and small. "I don't know them."

"Can you make it the rest of the way?"

I lifted my legs, testing. "Yeah."

"Go ahead," he said. "I'll follow along behind you."

I started walking, then jogging. Feeling was returning to my muscles. The white Toyota trailed me by twenty feet, half on the shoulder, its blinkers going. A car sped around us, then a pickup.

An old lady in a big brown car approached going the opposite direction and slowed, giving Rex the evil eye. I waved to her and tried to smile. She frowned and went on.

We got to my neighborhood. I jogged into my driveway and Rex pulled in behind me. He stayed in the car. His windows were down.

"This is my house," I said.

"Uh-huh." He was writing something on a notepad.

I breathed in the friendly, mist-drenched smells of lawn and bark dust and blue spruce.

Rex reached a piece of paper out to me. "This is the information to give to the police. A description of the car and the license number. Your dad should talk to them soon. Can you get in touch with him right away?"

I nodded and took the paper. "Thanks." At the bottom he'd written his phone number and name: Rex Rayburn. "I was scared," I admitted.

He smiled, comforting. I knew instantly what Megan saw in him: he cared. "I'm glad I came along," he said. "You take it easy, Casey."

He knew my name. Megan must have told him all about me, maybe pointed me out. Probably when the two of them were driving by, out on a date or something.

He backed out slowly and headed down the street. I walked out to the end of our driveway and watched him turn into Megan's.

Suddenly my knees felt as if they were being churned in a blender. What would have happened if Rex hadn't come by? Nothing, maybe. More words, more nastiness, and the mouth-breathers would've gone somewhere else to do their dirty work.

Or maybe something *would* have happened.

But I didn't want to think about that. I went in and called Dad and gave him the story. He was upset. He asked me if I was okay, and said he'd be home soon. I gave him a description of the guys and the information from Rex so he could call the sheriff. Then I went back outside on rubbery legs and flopped down on the grass.

Across the street, the workers' truck was parked in Autumn's driveway. I tried to think about the new court—about something besides red cars and scary guys. But I kept seeing the car and hearing the rumble of its engine. And over that rumble echoed the voices: *Need a ride somewhere, sweetheart? Thirsty, baby?* I wouldn't forget those voices anytime soon.

But I wouldn't forget Rex, either. He'd come along just in time. I wondered if I had room for a poster-size photo of him on my bedroom wall, right next to Lauren Jackson, Sue Bird, and Inigo Montoya. I'd have him in something more heroic than a white Toyota, though. I pictured him roaring through a curve in a silvery sports car, full of bad-guy-busting gadgets. If Megan had to have a boyfriend—other than Dad—maybe Rex would be okay. Maybe. Dad would be my first choice, always.

I got up slowly and went to the hoop and began shooting soft, shaky, up-close jumpers. Right-handed.

"Casey!" I turned. Autumn was jogging across the street, dribbling a ball. My heart got lighter. She launched a thirty-footer that barely missed. "The court dudes are doing their thing," she said. "It won't be long."

"Great," I said, trying to sound enthusiastic, but I didn't fool her.

"What's up with you?"

While we shot, I told her what had happened.

"Scary, huh?" she said.

"I think I'll ride the bus from now on."

"We had guys like that in Seattle. Bad boys, trying to run your life. You can't let 'em."

"I should keep running to school?"

"Those guys can't be stupid enough to mess with you again."

I dribbled the ball hard right-handed, tattooing it against the cement. "You're right. They're not going to scare me into giving up."

Brave words. I didn't feel brave, but when I sat in the kitchen that night and told Dad that I wanted to keep running to school, he told me that Lainey Haller at the sheriff's office had said pretty much what Autumn had: the creeps wouldn't bother me again. But Dad didn't seem all the way convinced. Eventually we came to an agreement: I'd keep running, but he'd follow me in his car both ways, at least for a few days.

He studied the piece of paper Rex had given me. "Your Good Samaritan—Rex Rayburn—have you seen him before?"

I hesitated. "Yeah," I said finally. "I saw him at Megan's once." I should have said more than once. I should have exaggerated and said *every day,* so Dad would pay attention. "He was just leaving when I got there."

Dad's eyebrows lifted, but not high enough for me. I wanted him to get excited and get up and call Megan and demand to know what was going on.

Instead he said, "Hmm." That was it. At least for a few seconds. Then he said, "Do you know why he was there?"

I shrugged. "I tried to play detective, but Megan didn't cooperate. I think maybe she's seeing him."

"Seeing him?"

"You know—going out with him."

"Really?"

I shrugged again. "Maybe."

"I owe him a thank-you." That was it. He owed Rex a thank-you. Didn't he care about what I'd just told him? He went to the kitchen phone and dialed. He began speaking, but I could tell he was leaving his thank-you on an answering machine.

I sat at the table and thought about where Rex might be. If he wasn't home, was he with Megan?

I called Lisa that night and told her what had happened on my run home. She listened breathlessly, no TV sounds in the background.

"You're running again tomorrow?" She made the question sound more like a statement: *you've lost your mind.*

"With my dad."

"You're not afraid?"

"A little." I remembered what Autumn had said. "But I can't let those guys scare me out of living my life."

.

"You want me to run with you?" she said, barely loud enough for me to hear.

"I'll be okay. Dad's skinny, but he's like a mother bear."

She giggled.

"With glasses," I said, choking down a giggle of my own. But it was too late. I couldn't stop laughing. I didn't want to stop. I wanted to drown out those running-home sounds—music, car engine, voices— still echoing loudly in my head.

## ∾ *9* ∾

# Grit

The next morning Dad gave me a form showing he'd deposited the ten thousand dollars in my fund. Every year he'd shown me a receipt, even back when I barely had a clue what it was. He wanted me to know what was going on, but I could have done without thinking about it again. It was hard eating my cold cereal when my insides felt all twisted up.

The run to school started out scary, even with Dad's Jeep idling along fifty yards behind me. But I kept checking back, and he kept coming, top down, ready for anything, and I began to relax. After a while I got used to the occasional car accelerating around him, and before I knew it I was there.

That afternoon Dad was waiting for me when track practice ended. I gave him my backpack and bag and led him out of the parking lot. I felt a little silly with him shadowing me—kind of like I was ten years old again—but really I was glad he was there.

Nothing happened on the run home, except the farther I ran, the looser and quicker I felt. And by the time I reached my street, the ball seemed like it was strung to my right hand—going down, coming up, no peeking, automatic.

There was no white car in Megan's driveway. I stopped, and I hoped Dad would stop, too, but he kept going. Had he just given up on Megan?

I went in and told Megan and Dulcie my story. Megan acted like she hadn't already heard, but she didn't fool me.

I'd never known Megan to avoid the truth before. What was she trying to keep from me? Why didn't she talk to me about Rex?

It really was news to Dulcie. None of her wide-eyed emotions were faked. Maybe Megan hadn't told her because she didn't want to frighten her. But by the time I'd guessed at that, I'd already opened my mouth, I'd already let her hear the shakiness in my voice when I talked about the guys in the red car.

I headed home for a snack and homework. Then it was time for basketball practice. The Sorcerers— my team!

Dad took me to the ferry; Duncan picked me up on the mainland side and drove me into Seattle to meet Autumn and the rest of the team at Jefferson Middle. Vanessa was down at the far hoop again when we arrived. Autumn and I went down to tell her hi.

"Hops," she said, nodding to Autumn, then glanced at me. "Casey." It was the first time she'd said my name.

"How are you, Vanessa?" I said.

"Gettin' better." A girl of few words, but I was beginning to see she was that way with everyone.

She went back to what she'd been doing, a figure-eight, through-the-legs ball-handling drill I'd learned at camp and perfected at home. I got into position and started the same exercise, slow and deliberate at first, then faster. I whipped the ball through and around my legs so fast it was a blur. I didn't look in her direction, but I wondered if she was watching.

The other girls showed up, and we started our drills. I felt more comfortable. Now I knew names, and I knew what my teammates could do. I knew more about myself.

We ran through the offense. It started to click for me. We worked on defenses—half-court man and zone, trap, full-court presses—and I didn't feel lost.

Duncan put us through exercises where we had to use our off hand, and I did okay. But the other girls looked as if they'd been born ambidextrous.

With twenty minutes to go, Jimmy chose sides for scrimmage, five on five. Sink or swim time, I told myself.

But with Vanessa in my face, I couldn't make myself use my right hand. I tried to tell myself that it was all in my head, but the scar was still there, reminding me of how long I'd let my right hand just hang out. So I dribbled left-handed, passed left-handed, shot left-handed. And struggled. Every time I tried to drive, Vanessa overplayed me to my left, forcing me away from the basket, daring me to go right. I tried to move without the ball, run her off screens, get in the clear for passes. But I knew I was shortchanging myself.

The high point of the scrimmage for me was stealing a pass at half-court. I went all the way for a reverse layup with Vanessa shadowing me and swiping at the ball. It dropped in. I looked up and both coaches were smiling.

I also had a low point. I was dribbling left-handed up the left wing, with Vanessa forcing me to the sideline. Heading for no man's land in the corner, with no one to pass to, I decided I'd had enough. I crossed over to my right hand.

But the ball never arrived. Vanessa snaked in an arm, as if she'd been waiting for that move, and picked me clean. She went coast-to-coast, dropped in a high layup, and I fouled her. She gave me a smile when she went to the free throw line. I decided to believe it was a friendly smile.

After the scrimmage, Duncan took me aside. I expected him to get on me about losing the ball. "I was a little disappointed in you for a while, Casey," he said. "Vanessa was pretty much making you go where she wanted."

"I know," I said. "She plays good defense."

"She does," he said. "That's a big reason she's a starter. But you were making it easy for her."

"Swimming one-handed," I said.

"That's right. Hopin' to get somewhere but only treadin' water."

"Yeah," I said. There was no hiding in basketball. I thought of the clumsy crossover move and waited for him to bring it up.

"That's why I was so happy to see that crossover toward the end," he said. "A little smoother—just a hair—and you would've had her. Because she was way overplaying you. She was giving you a big alley to the hoop and you tried to take it. She was just quick enough to snag the ball."

"I need to work on it."

"Sure you do. Practice it at home, perfect it in the gym. A move isn't any good unless it's been hardened by fire. So be encouraged, not discouraged. Nothing bad happened, 'cause in practice only good things happen. Next time, she'll have to play you more honest, 'cause next time the move will be smoother. The time after that it might work."

I thought about what he was saying. If losing the ball in practice wasn't a big thing for him, why should I worry about it?

"Okay?" he said.

"Okay."

"Good for you." He eyed my elbow, and without thinking, I angled the scar away from him. "Accident?" he said.

"A car accident," I said. "When I was little."

"The one that took your momma?"

I nodded.

"Sorry," he said. "Does your arm still bother you?"

"Just in my head." I didn't want an excuse. I didn't want Duncan to think I had something I couldn't overcome. I wanted to forget that scar and all it stood for.

He studied my face for a moment, a little bit of frown in his eyes, as if he didn't quite believe me. Finally, he smiled. "I like your grit."

"Grit?"

"Pluck. Spirit. Stick-to-itive-ness. Grit's a good thing."

"Okay," I said. "Thanks."

The rest of the team was shooting free throws

at both ends. I joined Autumn's group. I hit eight in a row, each followed by a double clap from my four teammates lining the key. It sounded like a whole crowd of people. Finally I clunked one. The girls booed me.

But they were smiling when they did it.

# ❧ *10* ❧

# Duel on the Track

Wednesday arrived cool and drizzly. I hoped it would stay that way. I ran better under clouds. I was torn: run to school, or catch the bus; improve my basketball, or save myself for the big district meet that afternoon?

In the end I decided a slow jog wouldn't tire me out for races that weren't happening until nine or ten hours later. So I ran, dribbling the ball, one eye on traffic, both ears tuned to the comforting sounds of Dad's car on my tail.

I'd qualified for the final meet in three events— the 400 and 800 and the 4 X 400 relay— but I couldn't scrape up much confidence. The competition was fierce—the best girls from each of the five other schools in our league. They were all shorter than me, but they seemed older for some son—makeup and muscles and boyfriends hanging around. One of them was Lindsay Blake from Granite Falls, who'd never lost a race. Yikes!

The meet was held at Coupeville High School's sports field, a half-hour bus ride up the island. The black artificial track looked kind of old and worn, but its surface was smooth and it was six lanes wide, unlike the skinny ribbon of gravelly dirt at Langley Middle School. A crowd of people had shown up to watch. The sun was poking through, but behaving. A steady breeze swept across the wide-open field.

I ran a good 400—sixty-three seconds flat, a personal best for me—but came in third. Close, but third. Lisa took fifth. By the time the 800 came around, I was feeling jumpy and alone, even though Lisa was right there with me. Lindsay Blake—almost my height, lean, grim-faced—stretched and pranced in place a few feet away.

They started us in a cluster. When the gun went off, I held back, not ready to challenge the three front-runners—Lindsay Blake and Lisa and another girl from Granite Falls—who surged to the lead shoulder to shoulder and held it ten meters in front of the pack. I kept my distance through the first curve, the backstretch, the next curve, and the beginning of the straightaway.

Ahead of me, the second Granite Falls runner

drifted back. I caught her on the outside just as the gun sounded to signal the start of the final lap. I sensed Lindsay Blake's strength, and Lisa struggling to stay close. But as they came out of the turn, Lisa lost a step, then another, and another, until she was halfway between me and the leader.

I was still breathing easily, but with fifty meters of backstretch to go, my side started complaining. I tried to ignore it, concentrating on Lisa's back. I'd have to catch her first, then worry about Lindsay Blake.

The wind picked up. I leaned into it, staring at the scoreboard, imagining I was older and tougher, running for South Whidbey High against Coupeville.

High school runners didn't surrender to pain or wind.

We hit the curve. I couldn't hear anyone behind me. I couldn't hear anything but the in and out of my breath, the pounding of my heart, the drumming of my shoes on the rubbery surface.

I got ready to make my move. I shook out my arms and began pumping them back and forth like pistons—slowly at first, then faster, and faster, my legs moving with precision, my breathing in rhythm with my body. Time to dig deep.

Lindsay Blake came out of the turn accelerating, pulling away from Lisa. But not pulling away from me.

I caught Lisa seventy meters from the finish, cruising past her in lane two.

"Eat her up, Case," she gasped.

I didn't reply. I'd save my breath.

I lowered my head, kicked my body into high gear, and the gap narrowed to eight meters, then six, then four. Lindsay Blake glanced around and lost another step, and now I was close enough to see the sweat on her back. The pain in my side deepened. It spurred me on.

And now the wind was at my back.

With twenty-five meters to go, I pulled even. I heard shouts from the crowd on both sides of me. I heard my name. I thought I heard my dad. But my eyes stayed on the finish line, on the tape stretched across the track.

For a moment Lindsay Blake hung in, her long stride chewing up big chunks of track. But I dug deeper, pushed harder, and pulled away. I broke the tape by myself, staggered, and glanced back just in time to see Lisa nip Lindsay Blake at the line. Lisa had come back to take second.

We hugged, leaning on each other. I told myself I wouldn't doubt her dedication again. She had guts, and whatever training methods she was using—slow miles on the road, TV-watching, whatever—seemed to be working.

"I fed off your energy, Case," Lisa gasped.

"You've got grit, Lisa," I said.

She gave me an exhausted, quizzical smile.

"Grit's a good thing."

I looked up at the stands, imagining Mom's face in the crowd, imagining what she would think. The pain in my side was gone.

We didn't have much energy left for the relay. I ran anchor. I couldn't chase anyone down, but I managed to hold my position. We took third, which was pretty good for a team running on empty. At the finish line, Coach Dillard talked about effort and potential and how we were going to blow everyone away once we got to South Whidbey High.

Dad, Megan, Dulcie, and Lisa's mom came down and congratulated me and Lisa and the rest of the relay team. I got hugs from Dad and Megan, but Dulcie patted me hesitantly on the back. "Eww!" she said, wiping her hand on Megan's shorts.

Megan handed me a bottle of cold water and I took a long, thirsty swig, glancing around. I spotted a familiar face at the top of the bleachers. Autumn, along with her mom and dad.

I couldn't believe they'd come. I waved and they waved back and began making their way to the track. "Come on," I said to Lisa. "Let's go talk to our fans."

*"Your* fans," Lisa said. "I'll just hang out here."

And she did.

# ❧ *11* ❧

## Sink or Swim

**F**riday's practice went better. I forced myself to try out my right hand during our scrimmage and felt only half-awkward. I got the ball swiped only half the time. And I felt more a part of the team.

At the end of practice Duncan got us together and reminded us of the tournament the next two days—Saturday, and if we did well enough, Sunday. Top teams from around the Puget Sound area, some of whom the Sorcerers had played during their regular season, were entered. All were a mystery to me. I wondered how much I'd get to play.

Jimmy seemed to guess my thoughts. "Everyone plays on this team," he said. "So our first goal for this weekend's tournament is for all of you to use your playing time to get better as individuals.

Second, we need to improve as a team. Think of this as a warmup tournament. We gotta use these games to see what we need to do in the following two weeks to get ourselves ready to win the big one so we can move on to Iowa City."

Iowa City? Not New York or California? The national championships were in Iowa City? A warm, tingly feeling washed over me, head to toe. My imagination started working. If we went, I could see Mom's old school. I could breathe the air she breathed.

"I won't lie to you," Duncan said. "Coach Jimmy and I would like to win this thing. But we already have a spot in the state tournament, so losing won't hurt us. I'm more interested in how well you're playing, win or lose—your ability, court smarts, effort. Those things will go a long way toward telling us how much we should play you, especially when it comes down to crunch time."

Duncan had mentioned effort. I could do effort. I might miss shots and make bad passes and dribble the ball off my foot, but I could always fly around, work my tail off, grab rebounds, make life miserable for the other team. If the coaches wanted effort, I'd give it to them.

Our first Saturday game was early—9:00. We had to be at Jackson High School in Mill Creek by 8:15, which meant I had to be up by 6:15.

That didn't bother me. I was awake at 5:30, sitting at my window watching the sun come up, thinking basketball. I flopped on my bed and looked at Mom's pictures, wishing she could sit in the stands in a few hours and watch me take the floor in my cool blue uniform with some of the best girl basketball players in the state. I wondered if she would see me, the way people said: looking down from heaven, or standing beside me like a guardian angel.

Sometimes when I went to bed at night I concentrated on her picture, trying to carry the image over to my dreams. Most of the time it didn't work. Most of the time I had regular jumble-wacky dreams. But once in a while I'd have a Mom dream. I'd dream there'd been an accident, but she'd survived, and she was okay, and we were together as a family. She'd talk to me, and I'd talk to her, and I'd get this big balloon of happiness in my chest I'd wake up with in the morning.

And then the disappointment would come, like the slap of a wet towel. It was just a dream, after all.

I got dressed, grabbed my gym bag, a banana, and some granola bars, and hopped into the Jeep with Dad. We had twenty minutes to get to the next ferry. I used the time to talk to myself, to try to settle myself down. I was used to playing for fun. This would be fun, too, I told myself, just a different kind. I would be okay.

Our first game was against a team from Tacoma called the Intruders. They looked smooth during warmups. They ran their drills with precision, as if they'd done them a thousand times before. But we looked just as smooth. And bigger.

We huddled by our bench before the tipoff. I got the tight whirlpools in my stomach, even though I wasn't going to start and I didn't know when I'd get in. They said everyone would play, and that meant I had to be ready.

DJ jumped center for us. She got the tip to Vanessa, who hit Autumn streaking down the right side. One of the Intruders cut her off near the key, but Autumn crossed over, blew by her, and reversed in a left-hander off the glass. Picture perfect. Our crowd—small but lively—went wild. Dad was on his feet, clapping.

"A machine, baby!" Jimmy yelled.

The Intruders brought the ball upcourt. Duncan called out "Channel!"—our signal for our half-court trap. Rachel met their point guard near the jump circle and forced her right. Autumn trapped her at mid-court. She picked up her dribble and passed but Vanessa stepped in, quick as a cobra, and snatched the ball with a ten-foot lead on the nearest defender. She finger-rolled one in.

The Intruders' coach called time. Our crowd cheered. Our players sprinted to the bench.

"Use the backboard next time," Jimmy told Vanessa.

She gave him a look. "I made the shot."

"Doesn't matter, 'Nessa. We go with percentages, not what's pretty. Okay?"

Vanessa nodded. The coaches rattled off what they wanted us to do: trap, full-court press, drop back, alternate the defenses, keep them off balance, do the unexpected.

And we did. With two minutes to go in the quarter we were up by twelve, seventeen to five, and they'd gotten three of their points on free throws.

I was still on the bench. "Casey," Duncan said.

I popped up and crouched in front of him, my heart thumping.

"In for Vanessa," he said. "Wing. You know who she's guarding?"

"Number twenty-two," I said.

"Good," he said. "Work hard."

I checked in with the scorer. One of the Intruders threw the ball out of bounds. The whistle blew. The ref motioned me in. I told Vanessa she was out. She hesitated just a little before she trotted away.

Effort, I told myself. I inbounded the ball to Cristina and headed upcourt. I'd played a lot of basketball, but this felt like the first time.

I took my spot. They were running a man-to-man

defense. We went into our man offense. I worked through it, cutting, screening, taking a pass, giving one up.

Suddenly Carley set a perfect screen for me. I broke to the hoop, and Autumn hit me with a pass in full stride. Without putting the ball on the floor I went up and banked it in. The only better feeling would've been if I'd done it right-handed.

I couldn't help myself. I pumped my fist, looking for Dad.

"Channel!" Jimmy shouted. I sprinted to my spot, but I was late.

A shot went up from their wing. I raced to the boards, watched the ball carom off, and went up for it. From out of nowhere a long arm shot in front of me. DJ snatched the ball out of the air and fired an outlet pass to Autumn, who took one dribble and lofted the ball to Cristina. She went unchecked to the hoop. We were up by sixteen.

The Intruders' coach called time. He looked puzzled.

We added to our lead. I didn't come out until nearly halftime. I'd never worked so hard. I had six points, two fouls, a couple of rebounds, a couple of steals. I'd used my right hand a few times—not under pressure, but at least I'd used it.

By halftime we were ahead 43-14. In the second half, we didn't press, trap, or fast break. Duncan and

Jimmy wanted us to work on our half-court offense and not run up the score.

We won, 75-35. Our coaches were happy, but they said it was just a start. The Intruders didn't compare to some of the other teams we'd be facing.

But it didn't matter. I'd done okay, I'd gotten the first game out of the way. I felt less like an outsider and more like a Sorcerer.

We scouted the next game. We'd be playing both teams to get out of our bracket. One was tall, one was quick. The quick team won by three.

We returned from lunch and warmed up for our 1:00 game. We were matched against the quick team, the Sparks. They were from south Seattle, and some of our players knew some of theirs.

They didn't look impressive during warmups. They were all in that five-five to five-nine range, and their shots were a little off.

Once the game started, though, we were in a battle. When Megan and Dulcie walked in with three minutes left in the quarter, the Sparks were up, 12-9.

Duncan called time. He subbed in Cristina, Thea, and Carley. "They like to run," he said. "So let's slow it down and pound it inside. Hustle back into our half-court defense—two-one-two zone with DJ in the middle, Autumn and Cristina at the wings, Carley and Thea underneath."

Play resumed. DJ missed a short turnaround jumper but Carley snatched the rebound and put it in. We cheered as the team set up the zone, a scrambling picket fence around the key, with DJ in the middle like a big guard dog.

The Sparks coach yelled instructions. "One-three-one! High post! Movement!" But his players couldn't shed Autumn and Cristina. When they did, they couldn't pass inside, they couldn't get around DJ, they couldn't drive the baseline on Carley and Thea. They forced up shots from outside. We led by seven at quarter-end.

Sara and I went in. Carley intercepted a pass and hit me on the run. I spotted Cristina streaking for the hoop and looped a pass in front of her. She rocketed up for a layup.

The Sparks hurried the ball upcourt. Their point guard shouldered past me, but I stayed close, and when she went up for a shot, I went up with her. I swatted the ball cleanly, saw Carley gather it in, and raced upcourt. I glanced back as Carley launched a pass. I caught it, took two dribbles, and leaped high for the layup—right-handed—with a Sparks player riding me. The ball dropped in; the whistle blew. Foul.

The Sparks coach called time. I got high-fives from everyone. "Prime-time play, Casey," Duncan said. "Look for them to make adjustments," he told us, "but otherwise just keep doing what you're doing."

We did. Their adjustments didn't work. We won, 72-49. I scored eleven, my first game in double figures. After the game, after we exchanged attagirls with the Sparks, their coach came up to me and smiled and offered me his hand and I shook it. "Strong game, thirty-three," he said.

I couldn't believe it. *I* was thirty-three. "Thanks."

"I thought I knew the Sorcerers," he said. "Where'd Duncan find you?"

"Whidbey Island."

He shook his head. "Who'da thunk it?" He started away, but turned back. "Keep up the good work. Just not against us."

Duncan walked up, half-grinning. "Next thing you know, Buster will be sending you candy, trying to lure you away. But I'm glad you're with us."

I was, too.

Our last game of the day was at five against the big team, the Storm from Bellingham.

The game started. Suddenly we looked like we'd all learned basketball individually through some Internet course that didn't require us to actually play the game. Halfway through the first quarter, with the score even at nine, Duncan called time. His face was red as he stood and glared at the players coming back to the bench. His knuckles were white against his clipboard.

"Not enough lunch?" he said when we'd all gathered around. "Or are you girls just feeling generous? Or lazy? Or selfish? This is a team. You play like this in two weeks and it's gonna be a real short tournament and a real long summer. The Storm girls are playing with their hearts. Where are yours?" He looked from face to face. Quiet. Deep breaths. Downturned eyes. "Starters stay on the bench and watch. Next five, check in."

I couldn't look at the starters. The horn sounded. Jimmy stopped us as we headed to the floor. "Full-court, man-to-man D," he said. "Play with your hearts."

Cristina got me the ball on the right wing. I slipped Carley a bounce-pass inside. She made a beautiful move to the basket ending with a left-handed reverse layup. We pressed full-court. Cristina intercepted the in-bounds pass and hit me underneath. I banked in the shot, and suddenly the energy level changed. I heard our bench and fans waking up.

The Storm inbounded the ball, but we were everywhere. The thirty-second horn blasted before they could get off a shot. Turnover. Carley scored again. We rebounded a hurried shot at their end and Thea scored. They threw it out of bounds. I scored, out of our offensive set. We stole the ball and Cristina scored on a drive.

Finally they broke our press and scored, but we came right back. By the end of the quarter we were up by fourteen. We'd scored twenty-eight points in a quarter. We went back to the bench to cheers and high-fives. I smiled up at Dad and Megan and Dulcie.

The coaches left us in. With four minutes to go in the half, we had a twenty-point lead. Finally the starters returned.

They played hard, extending the lead. The second half we worked on our offense and tried different things defensively. I tested my right hand, having to think about it, but less. We won by thirty-something. I finished with thirteen, my high game so far. But according to Carley's mom, who did our stats, I had five rebounds and three steals, and I was prouder of those than the points. I wasn't proud of my two turnovers.

I felt pretty hyper on the drive to the ferry. But by the time we rolled onto the big boat and parked, I was nodding off. Dad kept talking, but it was like listening to a far-off radio station, fading in and out.

"We're home, kiddo," I heard him say from a distant somewhere. I felt his hand on my shoulder and opened my eyes to the inside of our garage.

I dragged myself into the house. But before I could start up the stairs, Dad stopped me. He gave me a hug and held on. "I'm proud of you, Case," he said. "Not just because you played well. But because you had the nerve to give this thing a try, and because of how well you've fit in with the other girls."

How well I've fit in. I decided Dad was right. Nine new teammates and only a minor bump or two in the road. I hugged him back, tight.

By Sunday, only four teams remained in the tournament. We opened up at noon against the Mountaineers, a team from Olympia. We hadn't seen them play and we didn't know much about them, except they were undefeated in the tournament, winning by an average of twenty. Scary.

The Mountaineers had a tall center, but their star was Brooke Lockwood, a shorter, wider, red-haired girl. She was quick and strong and could shoot. And their other players did a good job of getting her the ball. She got five of their first six baskets to keep them even. Ashley, trying to guard her, picked up two quick fouls and went to the bench.

The quarter ended with them up, 17-16. Only Cristina and Carley had subbed in, but I didn't mind. The intensity level had gone way up. So had my anxiety.

It's only a game, I told myself.

"Let me have her," DJ said to Duncan when our players got to the bench.

"Okay, but we can't afford you getting into foul trouble." He looked at Autumn, then Vanessa. "You wings have to help DJ. If Lockwood gets the ball inside, I want you to double down on her. This is a team game."

"Brooke Lockwood *is* their team," Vanessa said.

"Let's change that," Jimmy said. "Deny her the ball. Make her pass when she gets it. Force their other players to play."

Our same five went out. Brooke Lockwood got the ball inside, but when she tried to dribble, Autumn pounced. She passed to Cristina, who hit Vanessa, who went to the hoop uncontested. We were off and running. We were up by eleven halfway through the quarter when Duncan sent Sara, Thea, and me into the game.

I was nervous, but at least we were ahead. And Brooke Lockwood was taking a breather. We increased the lead to fifteen by halftime. I took three outside shots and made two, one of them a three-pointer, but I had a couple chances to drive right and I couldn't make myself do it. I couldn't quite break out of my little shell.

I was on the bench for the start of the second half, knowing I'd be getting more court time if I could be more confident with my right hand. *Use it,* I told myself. The arm's not hurt anymore, it's not weak, it's just out of practice.

Brooke Lockwood came back in, but she couldn't do much. I could tell she wasn't used to playing like a regular human. By the end of the quarter, we were up by nineteen.

I started the fourth quarter. "Effort," Duncan said as we broke our huddle and took the floor.

Our first time downcourt, Rachel got me the ball on the left wing. My defender was overplaying my left, daring me to go right. I took the dare. I faked left, crossed over, and accelerated. She swiped at the ball but missed. I dribbled twice *with my right hand* and saw a defender leaving Carley to challenge me. I hit Carley with a perfect pass. She put it in. Our crowd cheered.

We won by twenty-five. I got attagirls from Dad and Autumn's mom and even Noah.

As I headed outside to get some air, Duncan stopped me. "Good job, today, Casey. Beautiful assist." He made a swimming motion, arms reaching out strong.

I grinned. "Thanks."

## ∽ *12* ∽

# The Butterfly

We had less than an hour to savor our semifinal victory over the Mountaineers. Our last game of the tournament—the *championship* game—was at 2:30 against the Nightingales, a team from Vancouver, Washington. Autumn psyched us up for them by giving us little press-on tattoos of Mickey Mouse in his sorcerer's clothes. Everyone applied them to their left cheek. Except me. I put mine on my right. I needed a reminder: right hand, right hand, right hand.

We hadn't seen the Nightingales play, but the bracket results posted on the gym wall showed us something chilling: they hadn't had a close game. Ever. None of their opponents had even scored forty points. According to some girls who'd played them, they had a do-everything girl who played like a boy.

She was at most six feet tall, but she could grab the rim. In one game she'd blocked seven shots. Her name was Teresa Bonilla, but her nickname was "la Mariposa"—the Butterfly.

We'd only been warming up a minute when Duncan called us back to the bench. "What's the attraction on the other end?" he said.

We knew what he meant. We'd been spending every spare moment staring at the Nightingales, waiting for the Butterfly to do something spectacular.

It hadn't been hard to pick her out. She was cheetah-quick, with an explosive first step on her drives. She could go high to the hoop with both hands, stop and pull up on a bumblebee's eyebrow, hang in the air like she was on strings. To top it all off, she was beautiful, with olive skin and high cheekbones, shiny black hair pulled back in a long ponytail, and a smile that sparkled. She looked like she had no cares. Like she was expecting to have a wonderful time.

"She's a special player, but we have special players, too," Duncan said. "A lot of 'em."

"She should be lookin' at *you*," Jimmy said.

I wasn't so sure. But we put our hands together and yelled "Sorcerers!" as if the name could cast a spell, as if it could ground the Butterfly. We didn't peek again, at least I didn't, but a few minutes later the crowd whooshed, as if the air had been let out of them. The Butterfly had done something. I snuck a glance just as she released her grip on the rim and floated to the floor. A ball was tucked in the crook of one arm, a big smile lit her face.

Autumn got the assignment nobody else wanted: Teresa Bonilla. "Everyone has to help," Jimmy said in our pregame huddle. "You can't leave Hops high and dry or the whole team's gonna suffer."

La Mariposa jumped center and got the tap. The ball came back to her on the run and she knifed inside before we could react. She went high, finger-rolling it over the rim.

"Help!" Duncan shouted. "You need to help!"

They pressed us. Teresa played the middle, darting everywhere. She stole the ball on our first two attempts to bring it upcourt. Once she scored on a pull-up jumper from the free throw line, once she bulleted a pass to a teammate for an easy layup.

Duncan called time. The starters sat, stung. He knelt with his clipboard. "Here's what we're gonna do." He explained how to set up, where everyone should move.

We went back out. We got the ball in, we made short, quick passes, dribbling when we could. We got the ball into front court.

They were in a zone, Teresa patrolling the key. Ashley went up for a turnaround jumper, but from out of nowhere the Butterfly came flying to swat the ball out of bounds. We brought it in and fired it from side to side, trying to get their defense unbalanced. Autumn got the ball in the clear and let it fly. Swish! Three points. We'd cut their lead in half.

We pressed, but they broke it easily with Teresa dribbling hard up the middle, then hitting her post player for an easy eight-footer. Autumn was talking to Vanessa and DJ. I knew she was asking for help.

Rachel got the ball into DJ, but she hurried her shot, missed it, and the Nightingales came flying back. They bricked a shot, but the Butterfly raced in and tapped in the rebound. The crowd roared.

Duncan called time again. He told us we needed to use our size. Work the ball inside to DJ and Ashley, pump-fake the Butterfly, take the shot or hit an open teammate.

We settled down. We handled the press, ran our offense, used the clock, worked the ball inside, got the Butterfly up in the air. At the end of the quarter we trailed 19-11.

We went to a zone, with me, Carley, Cristina, DJ, and Thea.

The Nightingales subbed for Teresa, and without her they were a different team. We cut their lead to four. But a minute into the quarter the horn sounded. She returned.

We set our defense. The Butterfly rocketed past

me. DJ picked her up, but too late. Her soft floater swished through.

The ball came to me outside. I cast off, concentrating. Two points.

They scored. The ball rotated to me again, a little farther out. I shot. Three. The Butterfly hit a three with me almost hanging on her.

They went to a man-to-man defense. I attracted the Butterfly, and I couldn't shed her. She always knew where I was going, and she was constantly talking, sometimes in English, sometimes in Spanish. "Your shot looks so pretty, thirty-three," she said once. Then, loud, "Pero no vas a hacer otro." She smiled.

The Nightingales called time. On our way to the bench, I asked Cristina for a translation. She rolled her eyes. Her breath hissed out between her teeth. "She says you won't make another one."

Autumn replaced Thea, and I knew why. I wasn't scoring—the Butterfly was right—but I was keeping her busy. Autumn could operate with only a mortal guarding her.

She scored inside, then outside, then fed Rachel for two. The Nightingales didn't adjust, and Duncan left me in to cut and screen and loop.

At halftime we were down only 35-31. But their defense changed to start the second half: Teresa was defending Autumn; their point guard, quick and aggressive, had me.

It worked. Autumn struggled. I struggled. Their shots went in. Ours didn't. We couldn't get the ball inside. We had turnovers against the press. One of them was mine, when I gave up on my right hand and got cornered. Rachel twisted her ankle and had to go out. Vanessa fouled out trying to contain the Butterfly and went to the bench crying.

The Nightingales built a lead, and time ran out. We lost, 66-57. Even Mickey Mouse in his sorcerer's outfit hadn't helped us.

We got a little trophy for second place. Autumn and DJ made the all-tournament team. The coaches said that this was a good experience for us. That nine points was nothing. That we'd learned enough to make up that difference. That they'd do a better job of coaching next time. Because there probably would be a next time. Like us, the Nightingales were entered in the state championships in two weeks.

"You could be that good, Casey," Autumn told me as we watched the Nightingales celebrate. I knew who she was talking about, and I grinned, just a little.

I rode home with Dad, Megan, and Dulcie. We stopped in Mukilteo for Mexican food, my favorite, but I didn't have an appetite. I picked at my enchiladas and thought about things I should have done to help the team, mistakes I made, moves I didn't make. What could I do better next time?

I called Lisa. She was surprised that we'd lost. She thought we were unbeatable. And I guessed I'd been thinking so, too. I hadn't *considered* losing. I'd been thinking Iowa the whole time, like I was destined to see where Mom had gone to school. I thought about all the money Dad was setting aside for me for college. If we ended up not winning the next tournament, maybe I could take some of that money and pay for him and me to go back there, anyway. Maybe we could take Megan and Dulcie with us.

"I need to work harder," I said to Lisa. "Can I take you up on your offer—you know, to help me?"

"When?"

"The next two weeks. We have another tournament. The winner goes to nationals."

"What about Autumn? What about her new court?"

"She's busy tomorrow, meeting friends in Seattle. She gets home late from school every day. But she said we can use the court when it's ready."

"*We* can use it?"

"We. Autumn's dad wants us to."

"Your driveway's good enough," she said. "There's just two of us, right?"

"Probably. But Autumn's court will be the next best thing to being in the gym."

Lisa was silent on the other end of the line, but I could feel the reluctance humming through. Was she so jealous of Autumn that she didn't even want to use Autumn's court? "It's gonna have regulation backboards and baskets," I said. "Two of 'em. And a bigger, smoother playing surface with real lines." I waited for an answer.

"Okay," she said finally. "What can I do?"

"Anything. Play defense on me, let me defend you, get rebounds, feed me the ball on the perimeter, play bump, one-on-one."

"One-on-one?"

"Okay. No one-on-one."

"Tomorrow?" she said.

The next day was the Memorial Day holiday, a good day to sleep in. But I couldn't afford to sleep too late. I had to get better in a hurry. "I'll be ready by 9:00."

"I'll come to your house."

"Great." It would be double-good working out with someone. And more fun, even if it was Lisa the track athlete. I wasn't sure how much fun it would be for her, but maybe I could pay her back somehow.

I'd just hung up when Autumn called. She had something to show me.

She was out front when I got there. "Come on, tortoise girl," she said, heading for the backyard. She grabbed my hand. "Close your eyes."

The latch clicked. Autumn towed me along with my eyes shut tight while I imagined what I was about to see. I took small steps, unsure of my footing. We stopped.

"Open," she said.

I opened my eyes. The backyard had been transformed. A dazzling basketball court stretched out in front of me: dark green surface, all the right lines, high-tech backboards and baskets, nets that glowed, they were so white. It all made my driveway hoop look like something from a barnyard.

"It's beautiful," I said. "Awesome."

"The guys worked all weekend." She tossed me a ball. "I already christened the other basket. Noah's on a date, so he loses out."

I dribbled to three-point range. I faked left, faked right, and went up for a shot just inside the circle. It arced through, getting nothing but net. It was a delicious sound. The backspin carried it nearly back to me. "Not bad," I said, and we both laughed.

"Tomorrow," Autumn said as we walked off the court. "Be over here early. Stay as long as you want. No need to knock on the door. Just show up. If someone's home, it doesn't matter. To my family, basketball sounds are music."

"It's really okay if I bring Lisa?"

"Sure," she said. "Just tell her while she's in my yard, it's okay to smile."

I laughed, remembering Lisa's less-than-friendly attitude when she and Autumn had met. "I'll let you tell her that."

"I just might."

That night when I went to bed I stared at Mom's track picture. I wished I could show her Autumn's new court. I wished she could have seen the games and celebrated with me after the wins and most of all held me when we lost. I studied her face—the big, wide-set eyes, the turned-up nose, the smile. Did she dream about having a baby back then, when she was young? What did she think when I came into her life?

Outside, maple leaves brushed against the house like whispers. Friendly, spring-summer secrets. Mom, lulling me to sleep, I liked to imagine.

Who had taken her away from me? Had the guy who'd run us off the road all those years ago looked back to see what he'd done? Had I seen his face as his car skidded past us?

Try as hard as I could, I didn't remember. But maybe someday I would. I'd recall that one thing about him—pointy ears, a scar across a cheek, an extra finger on each hand, something ugly and scary—and I'd track him down. Like Inigo Montoya, I'd search high and low, and find him and bury my sword deep in his heart. And before he drew his last breath, I'd tell him who I was, and why he was dying. I'd have my revenge.

The Sorcerers' practice the next day was tough for me. Lisa and I had put in two solid hours of basketball on Autumn's court, then I worked on my own in my driveway and did a pile of homework. I had to fight to stay awake as I sat in Duncan's car. We talked basketball and worked our way through traffic to Seattle's Capital Hill neighborhood, where the coaches had found a grade school that would allow us to use its gym on the holiday.

But if Duncan and Jimmy noticed me dragging, they didn't say anything. Halfway through practice they called us to the middle of the court and talked about the Nightingales game, about the Butterfly. They asked for ideas on what we could have done better. Most of the girls came up with something— different defenses, different offenses, special plays, more shots inside, more shots outside, run more, run less. When it came to me, I could only think of one thing: "Play harder." The gym was hot. I was dripping sweat. "You guys—we—are better than they are. We just have to show 'em."

"Show 'em," Autumn echoed.

We knotted our hands in the center of the circle. DJ counted to three. "Show 'em!" we chorused.

I was dragging when I got home. Dad was in the family room with his two companions, the newspaper and the drone of the TV. He looked lonely. What would he do in a few years, when I'd gone to college, in a house filled with nothing but ghostly echoes?

I stood at the door, waiting. Finally he looked up, surprise in his eyes. "You snuck up on me, Case. How was practice?"

"Tough."

"That's good, right?"

I nodded and decided to get onto something I'd wanted to talk about for a long time, something that was bothering me right then, maybe because Dad seemed so alone. "Why haven't you ever asked Megan to go out with you?"

He stared blankly, like *Where did that come from?*

"Like on a date, just the two of you."

He made a show of studying his watch. "Shouldn't you be getting to bed?"

"I have time for an answer."

"An answer." He looked half embarrassed, half sad. I almost wished I hadn't asked the question. He pointed to the chair next to his. "Sit."

I scooted the chair closer and sat. He leaned back, as if trying to focus on my face. "Actually, I did ask Megan out. We had some dates."

"I don't remember that."

"You weren't around. You were at basketball camp, or sleeping over at Lisa's, or at someone's birthday party. We didn't want to make a big deal of it, or have you concerned. Dulcie wasn't old enough to know what a date was."

111

"But you didn't hit it off?"

He smiled. "I thought so. I had fun, she seemed to have fun. We'd known each other for years already. I'd seen her with you, with Dulcie. I knew she was kind and generous and compassionate."

"So you liked her?"

"I liked—more than liked—her. And I thought she liked me."

"But?"

"I don't know. Maybe I pushed things. One day I started talking about the future. I mentioned marriage. She acted like a deer in the headlights. The next day she told me she wanted to stop with the boy-girl stuff. She wanted to go back to being just friends."

"What did you do?'

"I tried getting her to tell me why, but she said she really couldn't explain it. Eventually I decided that she didn't want to hurt my feelings. That she loved me as a friend, maybe, but she wasn't *in* love with me. Which was hard, because by that time I was in love with her. It was hard to pretend to be just friends again, but that's what we did. We pretended. At least I did. And after a long time the pretending seemed real enough."

"So it's like it never happened," I said.

"There's a scar or two. But now she's the person who helped raise you. I'm the grateful dad down the street."

"I'm sure she's going out with Rex," I said. Sure enough, anyway.

"I think you're right."

"You do?"

"I mentioned his name to her after he helped you with the creeps in the car. She got this funny pink look on her face. She went quiet. I put two and two together. What you'd guessed then about them going out seemed to make sense."

"Aren't you going to do something?"

"Rex is obviously a nice guy," Dad said. "And Megan has the right to do what she wants with her life."

"You're not even going to try?"

Dad looked at me. He spread his hands in a kind of helpless gesture. "I did."

"You don't really care about her," I said. "When I'm gone you'll just have your stupid newspaper and the TV. You're gonna grow old and lonely." I waited a moment for him to say he did care, that he'd head over to Megan's and sweep her off her feet like the guys in the movies did. But he didn't say anything. He looked at me for a long time, then his sad eyes went back to his newspaper. I hurried from the room.

On Tuesday, I decided to stop by Megan's house on my run home. We hadn't chatted much lately, and I missed it. She'd always been interested in what

I was up to, what I was thinking. She'd taken me shopping, helped me with girl-stuff. But now I wondered if she was avoiding me. I didn't want to think about the reason.

There were no strange cars in the driveway. At the door I knocked my special knock. From the other side came the answering knock, and then Dulcie swung the door open, grinning.

"Mom!" she called, grabbing my hand, dragging me into the kitchen. Her homework covered the table. "Asey-kay's here, all sweaty!"

Megan leaned out of her office. "We like sweat in this house." She looked at me. "Come sit, sweetheart." To Dulcie she said, "You stay with that homework, slowpoke."

Dulcie made a sour face. I pulled up a chair next to Megan's desk and waited while she brought us lemonade. "Speak to me," she said, sitting. Her computer was on. She was working on a stack of files.

So I told her about school and practice and basketball stuff coming up. I told her when the tournament was, hoping she'd come. I mentioned— not too obviously, I hoped—that Dad was such a nice guy for letting me join the team and paying the money and hauling me to faraway places and watching my games even though I spent a lot of time on the bench.

She listened to everything, even my stories of

Lisa and how she was helping me even though she wasn't happy about the new stuff in my life. Megan was a good listener. She was usually a good talker. But this time she didn't volunteer anything, even when I ran out of words. "So that's all the news from the Wilde child. What about you?"

She looked at me as if she wondered what I was driving at. Then she told me how Dulcie was doing in school, how much she enjoyed seeing me play with the super team.

But she still didn't say anything about herself, and I began feeling frustrated. Megan, who had always been open with me, was suddenly closing up. But was she talking to someone else? Rex? Was she just leaving Dad and me in the dust?

I decided it was time to go. I was halfway to the street, looking back, waving to Megan and Dulcie, when the white Toyota pulled into the driveway.

I kept walking, dribbling my ball. The engine shut down. Rex got out, smiling a Brad Pitt smile.

"How you doin', Casey?" he said.

"Fine," I said. "Thanks." I walked around him, then decided I was being rude. I was being like Lisa—jealous. And I owed Rex way more than a bad attitude.

I turned back to him. "My dad told me the sheriff is tracking down those guys."

"How long will it take?" he said.

"I don't know. Dad says they're not from around here."

"Good," he said. "You take care, now." He grinned that grin, then walked over to Megan. He bent to kiss her, but she moved her head aside and stared at me over his shoulder. I knew I shouldn't be there. She looked away as Rex stooped to hug Dulcie. I hurried off, dribbling the basketball, hard.

The rest of the week was basketball, basketball, and more basketball. I loved it, and it kept my mind off other things. Lisa hung in there with me, even agreeing to long games of one-on-one, but by Friday she seemed less enthusiastic. "Tell me again what happens if you guys win the state tournament," she said as we left Autumn's yard in matching coats of sweat.

I was almost afraid to tell her. "Another month of practicing, then on to Iowa."

"Your mom's roots," she said. "Cool."

"More than cool."

"If you don't win?"

"We're through."

"Oh."

"You don't have to keep helping me."

"I want to. I want you to win. There just isn't much time for anything else."

"We'll have more time soon," I said. "Summer's coming."

"Yeah," she said. "And then *autumn.*" The expression on her face told me she didn't mean just the season.

Dad got a call from the police after he got home. They'd located the guys who'd harassed me. They were from Spokane, three hundred miles away. It had been a joke, they said, innocent fun. I didn't believe it, Dad didn't believe it, and the cops didn't believe it, either. They told the guys to stay far away or they'd find a reason to haul them in. I felt lighter-hearted. I said a prayer: Keep the bad guys off my road.

## ～ *13* ～

# Our Girls

**W**e Sorcerers practiced Saturday and Sunday. No one complained. We had to get better. And we'd all been playing long enough to know how you got better.

Lisa and I headed to Autumn's court after school Monday. We spent a long time working on my right hand. When we played one-on-one, I dribbled and shot only right-handed. And the more we played, the more natural it felt. I was getting there. But soon enough?

Dad was working on the computer when I got home. Which was a problem. I had an essay due the next day and I wanted to write it before I left for practice.

"Sorry, Case," he said. "I have to get this information together and fax it out. Pronto."

"I think I need my own computer."

"Christmas is coming." He looked at his watch. "I'll be done by six."

"I leave at six."

"Oh," he said. "Right. Sorry."

Not sorry enough to give up the computer. But I had another option. "I'll go to Megan's," I said. "She'll let me use her computer."

"Don't bother her if she's working."

"She said I could use it anytime I wanted." I could have reminded him that I had my own work file on Megan's computer, but I left in a small huff, grabbing my backpack on the way out the front door.

Megan's car was gone. No one answered the doorbell. But she'd told me I was always welcome even if she wasn't home. I got her key from the hiding place by the woodpile and let myself in.

The computer was on, with a new screen saver of me watching Dulcie turning cartwheels at Deception Pass.

I touched the mouse. The photo dissolved, and Megan's incoming e-mail page appeared. On top were a half-dozen messages she hadn't yet read, then a bunch of others she'd reviewed and saved. I took a quick look, curious about personal notes but trying not to be too curious. Based on the senders and subjects, though, the mail looked like work-related stuff, mostly.

Mostly. But one entry caught my eye. It had been sent a few weeks earlier by someone or something named Ex-ray. Not too unusual by itself. But the subject was on the strange side: "Our Girls."

Interesting. But I'd never opened other people's mail, paper or electronic.

I got to my file and started typing, putting everything else in the back of my head. I didn't have much time before practice.

I finished with about five minutes to spare, printed out the essay, and headed for the front door. When I opened it, Megan and Dulcie were standing there. Megan was fumbling for her key. "I saved you the trouble," I said.

She flinched; Dulcie squealed.

"Sorry," I said. "Dad was using the computer and I had something I had to get done, so I used yours. I was in a hurry to get to basketball practice."

"The computer?" she said, almost as if she'd never heard the word before. She hesitated. "Sure, Casey. I told you anytime, right?" She stepped in while I tried to slip out. Dulcie had fastened herself to my waist.

"I didn't touch any of your stuff." I wasn't sure why I said that. Being tempted wasn't a crime.

"I would never suspect you would," she said. "Not that anything of mine would interest you."

I wasn't so sure about that, but I didn't say so.

"I've gotta fly," I said to Dulcie. I squeezed her hard and she finally let go. I leaped from the steps and took off at a jog. "Thanks!" I called back over my shoulder.

"Practice hard!" Megan called back.

Tuesday crawled by. School ended, and I headed for home, jogging and dribbling, working on my right hand's memory. Megan and Dulcie were in their yard, weeding, when I got to their house.

Megan smiled, but there was something behind the smile I didn't recognize. Curiosity, maybe. Or suspicion. She stood and came close. I remembered when I was little and I thought she was a big lady. Now I was taller by a head.

"I'm glad you thought to use the computer yesterday," she said, and I wondered why she'd made the leap to that topic. Was she really glad? And if not, why not?

"It's nice to have a backup," I said.

"The big tournament starts when?" she said, but she was studying my face like she had a different question in mind.

"Friday," I said.

"I wanna go, Asey-Kay," Dulcie said in her loud voice. She stood and held out her hands and I tossed her the ball.

"Good," I said. "We need loud fans."

Lisa was working with me in my driveway when

Autumn and Noah came home. Suddenly I got an idea for a more worthwhile practice session, but it would involve Lisa having a change of heart.

"You wanna go see if Autumn and Noah are up for some two-on-two?" I asked her.

"That's okay," she said. "You go ahead."

"If I go by myself, it won't be two-on-two."

She looked across the street. Autumn and Noah were hauling their backpacks out of their car. They waved. I waved back, waiting for Lisa to do the same. And finally, just before Autumn and Noah turned and headed off for their front door, she raised her hand and did a little finger-wiggle.

"It'll be better than one-on-one," I said. "You'll have a teammate."

"Who?"

"I don't know. We'll figure it out."

"Who'd want me?" Lisa said.

"All of us," I said. "It's just so we can get better. Maybe you and Noah could be a team. We could switch it around after that."

She rat-a-tat-tatted the ball on the cement. She studied her watch. She took a deep breath. "Noah, huh?" She grinned a little bit.

"If we can get him to play."

"Okay," she said finally. "Anything for you."

I smiled, inside and out. "Let's go."

Autumn was sure Noah would play—he'd do

anything to postpone homework, she said—and she was right. And he didn't seem to mind having Lisa for a teammate.

"Lisa and Noah," he said, strutting onto the court. "The Dream Team." He tapped knuckles with Lisa, who turned a little pink. "Eat your hearts out, Sorcerers!"

We tried to ignore him, but it was hard. He started out guarding Autumn, then he switched to me. It was like the Butterfly was guarding me again, and at first I couldn't do a thing. He was in my face, quick-handed, quick-footed, swarming. I tried going right a few times and he swiped the ball and I stopped using my right hand. So he overplayed my left, daring me, and I took the dare. I crossed over and went right and past him, and when Lisa picked me up I hit Autumn under the hoop for an easy bucket.

"Nice move, Casey," he said. "Don't be shy with it."

"Sink or swim," I said, moving my arms through an imaginary crawl stroke.

He chuckled, as if he'd heard it a thousand times before. "Yeah."

He kept up the pressure, always shading my left, giving me my right, and I kept trying it, some-times successfully, sometimes not, but the more I tried it, the more I liked how it felt. Toward the end of our fifth or sixth game, Autumn passed me the ball at the top of the key. Noah came out to challenge me, close. I jab-stepped one way and went the other, slipping past him, going for the hoop. I went up, using my body to protect the ball. I felt his hand against my wrist, but I got off the shot. The ball banked in.

"And one," Noah said, admitting the foul. "Which hand?" He picked up the ball and flipped it to me.

"What?" I said.

"Which hand did you use for that deadly drive? The shot?"

I had to think. I didn't remember. I hadn't decided ahead of time and now I wasn't sure. I had to go back and picture my route to the basket, the way the ball angled off the board.

My right. I'd driven right, shot right. But the move had been automatic. I'd done it because it was the move to make. I felt myself grinning. I glanced at Autumn, at Lisa. They knew what I'd done, too. I looked at Noah. He looked serious, like a teacher. Laughing, I waved my right hand.

"Exactly," he said. "Don't think, just do."

Finally, we had to quit. Lisa headed home first, in a good mood but nervous about a big homework assignment.

"Thanks for the workout," I said to Noah as

Autumn began walking me to the gate.

"No problem," Noah said. "Lisa's my kind of teammate." He smiled. "She lets me do most of the shooting. And you're gonna be okay."

*Okay.* The way Noah said the word made me think he meant better than just okay. It made me feel good.

I'd just crawled into bed that night when Lisa called. "You really helped today," I said. "I'd still be treading water without you."

"You'd still have Autumn. And Noah. And your practices."

"Not enough," I said. "Not the same."

"Autumn's really good," she said.

"Yeah."

"And nice," she said. "You'd have fun with her in Iowa. I'm sorry I've been so…"

"It's okay." For a second or two, I was caught off guard. Lisa was saying good things about Autumn. "Iowa would be fun for me, especially," I said. "Because of my mom and everything." Then I had another thought: "Maybe you could go with us."

"Really?"

"Why not?" I said. "Families can go. I'm sure friends can, too. Especially really good friends. Best friends." I pictured everyone sitting in the stands in some huge arena, their voices cheering us on, Lisa on her feet, Dad next to her, Megan next to him, and

Dulcie, calling out my name in pig Latin in that fog-horn voice of hers. And what about Rex? Would he be there with Megan?

"I don't know," Lisa said.

"Plan on it. All we have to do is win the tournament."

"I guess I'd better keep helping, then."

We talked a while longer, and Lisa's voice told me she was excited about the possibility of going to Iowa with us. Finally, we said good-bye, and I lay there, waiting for sleep to come.

But it didn't. Something was bothering me. It was like having a name on the tip of my tongue. I had to come up with this thing or I'd be awake all night.

I concentrated, eliminating: school, the bad guys in the car, basketball, Lisa, Autumn, Dulcie, Dad—everything okay. Megan.

Megan. Megan was what was bothering me. I pictured her face the last time I'd seen her and the time before that. Not quite herself. Why? What was the deal with Rex? Was he her boyfriend or not? Why wouldn't she tell me? And why was she acting strange the day I used her computer and the next time she mentioned me using it?

Did she really think I looked at something I shouldn't have?

What would that something be?

I remembered the e-mail from Ex-ray, and the subject: "Our Girls." Whose girls? What girls? Megan had Dulcie, and sometimes she talked about Dulcie and me being her girls. But who would be the other half of the "our"? Who would have sent the e-mail?

Dad?

"Our girls" would make sense if Dad had sent the note. But why Ex-ray? Dad's name was always Keith, except once in a while when Dulcie got cute with the pig Latin. Then it was Eith-kay. Not Ex-ray. Ex-ray would translate to something else.

Rex. Ex-ray would be Rex.

I sat up. The solution to the puzzle wasn't on the tip of my tongue anymore. It had slipped back down and lumped in my throat. So Rex was writing to Megan? About "our girls?" What did that mean?

# ❧ *14* ❧

# The Message

**B**y the time I left school the next day I had a plan, but I didn't feel so good about it. The goal of the plan was to read Megan's e-mail, even though I'd just been patting myself on the back for never reading someone else's mail.

The first big test of my honesty, and I was about to flunk. For just this once, I told myself, I was going to put curiosity and a vague but strong feeling of unease—Lisa might have called it *intuition*—ahead of integrity. I just knew Rex's e-mail had clues to his puzzling relationship with Megan. And maybe me. I just knew something was wrong.

The plan was simple. I would wait around for Megan to make her daily run to the post office to drop off her mail. That usually happened after she'd wrapped up her work for the day, sometime between four and four-thirty. Once she was gone, I'd have fifteen or twenty minutes to get back into her house and see what I could see.

No one was in Megan's yard when I ran past, but her car was in the driveway. It was too early for her to leave. I'd be back.

I got home, pulled a school notebook from my backpack, and went back outside. I could see Megan's front yard, but not deep enough into her driveway. I walked across the street, dribbling my ball, to get a better angle. And from there I saw the back of her car. Now all I had to do was keep checking.

Time passed slowly as I shot and then dribbled back and forth across the street, watching. Too much time? Was she even going to the post office today?

Finally I heard a car start. Pretending to concentrate on my routine, I kept one eye on Megan's yard. And a moment later she backed out and drove off.

She was barely out of sight when I picked up my notebook and jogged down the street. I didn't have time to waste.

I got the key and opened the front door. The house was quiet inside. I could almost hear my heart pounding. I could certainly feel it. I sat down at Megan's desk with my notebook in plain sight, just in case she came back unexpectedly.

I moved the mouse, and the screen saver disappeared. I clicked on e-mail and it opened to the incoming mailbox.

She had a few new messages, but I ignored those. I scanned down to where I thought "Our Girls" had been the last time.

Not there. I scrolled farther. I scrolled all the way down and back again. Nothing.

Maybe she'd moved it to one of her other mailboxes. I checked "Job," then "Personal." Still nothing. And I didn't know what else to do. Megan had gotten rid of "Our Girls," though it looked like she'd left everything else.

Why? What was the message she was hiding?

I stared at the screen. If I was ever going to know, I'd have to ask her. But would she tell me? I didn't think so.

I checked my watch. She'd been gone ten minutes already. I needed to leave. I started to close the e-mail program when I realized there was one place I hadn't tried: "Trash."

I clicked on it and held my breath while it opened up.

A screenful of messages appeared—147 of them, according to the number at the top of the page—and the third one on the list was "Our Girls." She'd put the mail in "Trash," but not emptied it.

I clicked. It opened. I read.

"Megan—" it began.

"I know you're not 100% in favor of my move, but I promise not to cause you any problems. I think me being back here is going to work out best for the girls. The promotion means I can afford to give you more for Dulcie and our young friend. And I'll be able to see Dulcie once in a while, maybe, if we can figure out how to do that without upsetting her. I've already missed eight years of her life, and I'd like to at least witness the rest of it, even if I have to stand on the sidelines.

"I'm still doing some back-and-forth to the San Francisco office, so the postmark on C's package won't change this year. As always, let me know as soon as it arrives. I remain nervous about sending cash. I'll be in touch. *Rex.*

I had to get out of the house, but I couldn't make myself move.

All my energy was going to my brain, where my mind was racing, trying to digest what I'd just read. I clicked on the "print" commands and listened as the printer whirred into action, drowning out street sounds.

I struggled to my feet and hurried to the window. No car yet. Back at the desk, I closed Rex's message, switched from "Trash" to "In," and closed the e-mail program. Then I snatched the paper from

131

the printer. Everything was back in place.

Once outside, I felt almost normal. The sun was out, the air tasted fresh. Filling my lungs, I locked the door and put the key back in place. When I got to the street, I looked right and turned left. There was no one in either direction, and I started to run, trying to clear my mind.

Ten minutes later, I sat on my bed. I couldn't stop shivering. I was one of "the girls," the "young friend." I was "C." Rex had been sending the money. And Megan knew about it.

So Rex was Dulcie's father. Her runaway dad didn't live on the east coast somewhere, like Megan had said. He'd lived in San Francisco, and now he was living near us—maybe on the island, or close by.

Did this mean Rex had something to do with Mom's death? Was that why he was sending the money? And what did *Megan* have to do with this? Part of me wished I'd never opened the e-mail.

What would Inigo Montoya do now? What if there was no six-fingered man? What if the person who had killed his father was just a regular guy? A guy who'd helped Inigo out of a serious jam? Or not a guy at all? What if it was someone who'd raised him, someone he loved?

I sat for a long time. The house was quiet. The phone rang once—Autumn, telling me to be at her house at 6:00 to catch a ride to practice. I told her

I'd see her then.

But I didn't know how I'd make it through practice. The phone rang again. Lisa. Part of me wanted to hear her voice, the other part couldn't imagine having to talk. I didn't answer.

Finally I got dressed, went to the kitchen, and choked down some toast and peanut butter. I washed it down with about a gallon of water, but there was a bad taste in my mouth that wouldn't go away.

Practice felt like a disaster. I tried to listen, I tried to concentrate on what I was doing, but my mind wasn't on basketball. I missed shots, threw bad passes, plodded through drills, fell back into old, comfortable habits: left hand, left hand. I was relieved when the last whistle blew and I could pull on my warmups and go home.

Dad was gone when I got there. He'd left a note saying he had a late meeting. I had to talk to him, to tell him what I'd found on Megan's computer. But I didn't know if I should talk to him first, or Megan. It was too late to call her, anyway, and too late to go visiting. And what would I tell her? That my spying had paid off? That I didn't want to be around her anymore?

And worse—what would she tell me?

It was nearly midnight when I called Dad's cell

phone and got his voice mail. "Where are you?" I said, and hung up. I went to my room and turned out the light, but I had trouble getting to sleep. Sometime after I finally dozed off, though, I woke to voices. Dad and Megan were downstairs talking, loud enough for me to hear, not loud enough for me to understand. And the voices sounded different— angry. Dad's did, anyway. And he was doing most of the talking. Megan's words came in one- and two-word bursts. Finally he said something and I picked out my name from the jumble. I sat up and waited for Megan's voice, but it didn't come.

Then I heard muffled sobs. Going on and on. I went to my door and listened for a moment and crept out into the hallway and down the stairs.

Megan was on the living-room couch, curled up in a corner. Dad was on the other side of the room, sitting on the edge of a chair. He looked up at me.

"Casey," he announced, and Megan took her hands away from her eyes and focused in on me in the near-darkness of the room.

She picked up something from her lap. "You left this at my house, Casey." Her voice was gurgly and shaky. She was holding my notebook.

"I opened your e-mail," I said. "I read it."

"When you came back?"

"Yeah."

"I thought you might have seen it the first time

you came over, but you didn't act like it," Megan said, almost to herself. "I deleted it in case you came back and got curious. But I didn't empty the trash. I didn't think about it."

I glanced at Dad. He was scowling at the floor, then at Megan. I'd never seen him look at her—at anyone—like that before.

"It's probably for the best, though," Megan said. "I'm sure it is."

"I've said enough," Dad said to Megan. "Casey's here now. You need to tell her the whole story."

Megan sat up straighter. "Yes," she said. "I do. No sense in waiting. There never was."

She got up and moved behind the couch, leaning on it, as if she needed the support. "After I tell you, I don't expect things to be the same between us, ever. But your dad's right—you need to know, and I've had it weighing on me for too long."

"It's about Mom," I said.

"I'll start at the beginning." Megan took a breath. "Rex Rayburn and I met at college. We fell in love. At least we thought it was love. Halfway through my junior year, I came back home to help my mom, who was sick with cancer.

"My relationship with Rex turned rocky. One night—a rainy, nasty night—we had a short but ugly long-distance conversation. Rex had been drinking. He thought he needed to see me in person, and right away. He made it almost all the way from Bellingham to my house. He was speeding through a curve, out of control, when he skidded across the center line and forced your car off the road." She paused, looking at me. I stared at her.

"He was a mess—soaked, scared, almost incoherent—by the time he came to my door. He knew the accident was bad. He'd already called the 911 operator from a pay phone, but he didn't say who he was, that he was the driver of the car that had caused the accident. And he begged me not to say anything."

"And you just went along with it?" I said.

Megan nodded, barely enough to notice. "I thought he'd confess once he thought about it. At the time, I still thought we'd stay together.

"He went back to school, but by then we knew your mom had died and you were injured. He couldn't get through the semester. We drifted apart, or maybe we were pushed apart by what he'd done. He moved to California and found a job. I didn't tell him I was pregnant. I didn't want to complicate things even more.

"My mom died. I was lost—I missed her so much! Dulcie was born. Rex still didn't know about her. When I found out your dad was looking for a childcare person, I talked to him, praying he'd hire me. I had to do something for him, for you. And I needed money. He gave me the job."

I looked at Dad, sitting back, arms folded across his chest, distant now.

She went on. "One day when Dulcie was a few months old, Rex called me out of the blue. He wanted to know about you, and I decided to tell him about the baby, too. He was hurt that I hadn't told him, but he volunteered to start sending money for her. And he had two favors to ask. One, he wanted her photo. Two, he planned to give you money for college, to try to make amends in a small way. He asked me to let him know that the money was getting to you safely, since to remain anonymous he had to send cash.

"So I agreed to it. I thought he was doing something worthwhile, and I thought if I helped a little, I might feel less guilty. I knew Dulcie and I could use what money he sent. He wasn't making a lot then, but he went without in order to send us whatever he could afford. He lived in a cheap apartment, drove an old car, didn't buy things. As he made more, he was able to give more."

I tried to absorb what Megan was saying. It sounded like something made up, like it hadn't happened to me. I pictured Rex's face. How could he have run from the accident? How could he think money would make up for what he'd done?

"He'd call me a few times a year," Megan said, "sometimes about the money, sometimes about wanting to see Dulcie. To just drop by and see her without telling her anything. I sent him more pictures, I told him things about her, hoping to satisfy him, but it had the opposite effect. He started calling me more, talking more about visiting her. Finally a couple of months ago he told me he'd gotten a promotion to his company's Seattle office.

"I didn't know what to think. Dulcie knew she had a father, but she thought he was on the east coast somewhere. She'd never talked to him, and she was okay with that. But last month Rex moved nearby—to Mukilteo. He began catching the ferry over to see Dulcie. He didn't push it, he didn't tell her who he was. He knew I wasn't comfortable with him there. Seeing him just reminded me of what he'd done, what he and I hadn't done. I didn't know what to do.

"I should've finally confronted Rex. I should've told him I was going to the police. Or I should've just gone to them myself. But the night of the accident, knowing what he'd done, I'd let him into my house. What was I guilty of? And if I went to prison, what would happen to Dulcie?"

*We'd* take Dulcie, I wanted to say, but I couldn't imagine Megan sitting in a prison cell. I couldn't even think about it. I waited for Dad to say something, but he didn't.

Megan took a deep breath. "When I found your

notebook, I knew you'd been back. I looked at your work file and didn't see anything from today. I noticed Rex's mail was still in the trash, just waiting to be read, and I figured you'd done that. I felt sick. I knew you must be thinking the worst of me. I thought about telling more lies. But I knew where more lies would lead.

"I couldn't keep the story to myself anymore. I found a sitter for Dulcie. I told your dad I needed to talk to him." She glanced at Dad, who stared straight ahead, at nothing. His eyes were watery. "I've been in love with him a long time, Casey, but I couldn't let myself get close to him. Not when I was living a lie. When I finally told him the truth, he was nicer to me than I deserved."

She came out from behind the couch and stood, vulnerable, in the center of the room. "I'm sorry, Casey," she said. "About everything. I've loved knowing you—I love you! If only I could undo the last nine years."

Still Dad said nothing. "What are you going to do?" I said, finally.

"Tomorrow I'm going to talk to Rex," Megan said. "I'll ask him to turn himself in. I'll tell him that I'm going to the sheriff Monday, regardless of what he decides. I don't know what the laws are, but I know I didn't do the right thing. The sheriff might say I helped Rex, that I was an accessory."

She swiped at her face. "I should be going."

Dad stayed silent. I didn't know what to say. Hurry and go? Stay away? Stay? Megan turned and slipped from the room, a spirit of someone I'd known. Or thought I'd known.

I heard the front door close. "She said she loves you," I said.

"I heard her," Dad said. "I heard everything."

"The accident wasn't her fault."

"Not the accident." He got up and put his arms around me. "The lies, though...all these years."

Eventually I went back upstairs, hoping Dad wouldn't check on me. Three times I'd assured him that I was okay, but he didn't look assured. And if he came into the quiet of my room now, my heart was booming so loudly it seemed as if it would give me away. It would tell him I wasn't okay. I pushed the sleep button on my stereo, and the gentle after-midnight sounds of something new-age and spacey sighed from my speakers. My heartbeat—a drumbeat now, muffled—blended in with the music.

I lay back on my covers, blanketed in the glow of light coming through my window from the street lamp and the full moon outside.

What would happen to Megan? Would she go to jail? Even if she didn't, would she ever be a part of our lives again? Would Dad let her? Would I? Would I see Dulcie again?

I tossed and turned. What about Rex? What would he do once Megan told him she was going to the police? What would happen to him? Not a sword to the heart, but jail, probably. What he deserved. He seemed like a nice guy, but underneath the nice, what was he, really? He drove drunk, ran us off the road, ran away from the accident, never admitted it was his fault.

But that was then. What about the years since? He'd tried to make up for what he'd done. He'd sent money for me and Dulcie. Every year he sent lots of money for me, even when he didn't have much.

So? He was a killer. He killed Mom. Had he changed? Why hadn't he turned himself in? He deserved a sword to the heart. Thump, my heart went. Thump.

The light fell on the photos of Mom and her friends, Mom and me. What would she do? What if I'd been the one who died? Would she forgive? Where *was* the answer?

I stared at the photo of the two of us, blurring my eyes, pretending we were moving, she was singing to me.

I picked it up and swung my feet to the floor. I stood, swaying in place to the music, remembering something from long before. I was in Mom's arms, and we were in the living room, cheek to cheek, dancing. Circling and twirling and dipping.

I remembered her laugh, the way her head tilted back when that musical sound poured out. I remembered her smell, flowers and spice.

I moved across the floor, holding the picture to my chest, eyes half closed. The glow of moonlight and streetlight cast my shadow on the wall as I twirled slowly. I felt thick rug on the bottom of my bare feet, then wood, then rug again.

The music stopped. I stopped, still holding the picture close. Different music started, but I stood in one place, feeling the hard, cool surfaces of wood and glass. Not Mom.

I heard footsteps on the stairs and hurried to my bed. Dad knocked softly and came in. I faked sleep, breathing slow and even.

"Sorry, Case," His voice was soft and hoarse, worn out.

I breathed. In and out. Slow. Rhythmic. The room was silent, dark, cool. I drifted through the stars, hunting for Mom in every wrinkle of space, every glimmer of light. Why couldn't she be here right now, standing at Dad's side, waiting to dance with me?

He started to move away. "I'm awake," I said.

His fingers were light, brushing the hair back from my face. "You okay?" He sat on the edge of my bed and held my hand.

"Not sleepy."

"Want to talk?"

"He acted like he cared about me," I said.

"Rex?"

"He let me think he was like my guardian angel or something."

"I don't think he'll ever understand what he took from us," Dad said.

"She used to dance with me. I just remembered."

I thought I saw a smile on Dad's face. "You were quite a pair."

I closed my eyes and imagined the three of us— Mom and me dancing, Dad watching. She'd been gone nine years, but I still couldn't believe I'd never see her again.

"I used to ask her if I could cut in," Dad said. "She'd laugh and dance away, make me chase you."

I pictured it. I liked the picture. I squeezed Dad's hand and let go.

"Go to sleep," he said, getting up and moving off. "We'll work this out."

## ❧ *15* ❧

# Sharing the Weight

I woke up Thursday morning hoping Wednesday night had been a bad dream. But I knew the difference. The voices, the words, still echoed in my ears.

Downstairs, Dad asked how I was doing, but he looked preoccupied. His eyes were red and sleepless.

Before I left the house, he hugged me and ran his fingertips down my cheek, like he was making sure I was still in one piece. "Want a ride?" he said.

I held up my basketball. "Friday's coming."

Lisa and I sat in lounge chairs pulled close together on a patch of backyard grass. The sun was out, streaming through the trees, reflecting off the pond. Lilacs were in bloom, and the air smelled alive. I breathed deep, trying to figure out where to begin. Lisa was quiet, waiting.

"Ready for this?" I said.

I could feel her eyes on me. "It must be big."

"Yeah." It was big, and heavy on my shoulders, on my heart. I needed to unload, and Lisa was a person who would listen and understand and not share until I said it was okay.

I started out, not sure how to begin, but once the words came, they came fast. I told Lisa about finding the e-mail, about the conversation with Megan and Dad when the air we breathed was thick with feelings because of the thing with Rex that Megan had kept hidden for so long. I talked about Megan, how I felt like she'd betrayed me but I didn't want to lose her and now I was worried that Dad would hate her forever and she might even have to go to jail. And what about Dulcie? And Rex? How far would he fall? I should hate him, but I wasn't sure that's what I felt. I talked about Mom again, how I'd been thinking about her whenever I slowed down long enough to really think at all.

Lisa didn't say much. She asked a few questions and nodded and gave me tissues when tears spilled down my face. She listened like a best friend. When I was all done, she held my hands and let me cry.

"I think you'll figure out what to do, and this will turn out okay," she said finally. "It had to get out in the open." She looked at me steadily. "I'm glad you decided to talk about it. With me."

"Me, too," I said.

The coaches had scheduled an extra practice that night to get ready for the tournament. After Lisa left, I ate a peanut-butter-and-jelly sandwich, a banana, and some chocolate-chip cookies Megan had stashed in our freezer. I wondered if she would ever make us cookies again.

I left for practice. It was good riding with Autumn, being around her and Duncan, who didn't know anything about what was happening with me. They talked basketball, about how awesome it would be to get to nationals, they joked, they told stories.

I tried to think of basketball, only basketball.

An easy ferry ride, a tough struggle through traffic, got us to O'Dea High School, an all-boys' school on a hill above downtown Seattle. When we came in, Vanessa was working on moves to the hoop. "Springy floor," she said to Autumn and me. And it was. When we started warming up, I felt like I was getting higher, staying in the air longer. I thought about la Mariposa. Could she dunk in this gym? I pictured myself hanging on the rim. But the floor wasn't *that* springy. I'd have to wait a while, work a while, grow a little, maybe, before I did any rim-hanging.

"You're skyin'," Vanessa said after I went high for a layup.

"It's the floor," I said.

"Nuh-uh," she said. "You got some hops. You think so, Autumn?"

"Casey?" Autumn said, grinning, low-dribbling the ball around and through her legs. "I think we should start calling her the Moth."

"Yeah," Vanessa said. "She'd play real good in the dark."

I imagined myself as a moth, flitting around a light, bumping into it, getting burned, too dimwitted to leave. Not exactly the same image as a butterfly. I laughed. They laughed. I laughed some more. It felt good.

But once practice began, everybody was focused. We ran hard through the usual drills, the usual offenses and defenses. But the coaches threw new things at us, too. One of them was the box-and-one defense, where four players set up in a two-two zone and the fifth player targets the other team's best player man-to-man. As soon as we started running it, everyone knew who it was aimed at. And Jimmy confirmed it. "We'll call this the butterfly net," he said. "In case we have to face Ms. Bonilla again."

We ran it in half-court and off and on in the scrimmage. The coaches tried different people—Autumn, Thea, Vanessa, and me—in the chaser position. I liked running, denying the passes, sticking like sweat to the person I was guarding. And if she slipped past me, I liked having the zone to back me up.

Offensively, I had the best scrimmage ever. I used both hands without thinking about it. No one overplayed my left, no one crowded me and dared me to go right. So I had shooting room, I had passing room, and if a defender got close, I didn't hesitate to drive, either direction. Automatic.

I had my right hand back, and for the first time I felt whole.

The coaches noticed my play. We were shooting free throws after a water break, and I looked up and Duncan and Jimmy were smiling at me from the sideline. Duncan had his arms swimming through the air.

At the end of practice, the coaches got us together. They talked about getting sleep, eating right, staying healthy.

"After the Nightingales game, we weren't unhappy," Jimmy said. "Not with you guys, anyway. Because you did a good job of applying what you'd learned all year, and executing our strategies during the game."

"It was us—the coaches—who needed to give you a better plan," Duncan said. "And if we do, and you all keep your faith in us and improve your execution just a little, too, we're gonna be okay this weekend."

"No matter who we play," Jimmy said. "Butterfly, bumblebee, Batwoman, whoever."

"On three," Autumn said. "Execution." I thought of the other meaning of the word. I thought about Rex. And Inigo Montoya.

DJ counted to three. "Execution!" The sound echoed around the gym, reminding me of where I was, and what I really wanted to concentrate on. My heart filled my chest. Basketball, I thought. If everything else crumbles, I'll still have basketball in my life. My now very sorry life.

## ❧ *16* ❧

# Bad Guy

The tournament began Friday night at Juanita High School, across Lake Washington from Seattle. Some of the cars in the crowded lot had writing—team names and cities—on their windows. As Mrs. Hopkins searched for a parking spot, I saw Bellingham, Wenatchee, Yakima, Tacoma, Olympia. Spokane, home of the creepy guys. I didn't see Vancouver, but I knew the Nightingales would be there. I knew the Butterfly would be floating.

Autumn, DJ, Vanessa, Carley, and Rachel were already there when we got inside. We girls talked and tried to relax as the courts were set up and swept down for the games—four at 6:00, four at 8:00. By the end of the evening, eight teams would have a win and eight teams would already be in a hole, scrambling to get out. I didn't want to be in that hole, and looking around at my teammates, I could see no one else did. All of them were wearing their game faces.

When everyone had shown up, Rachel pulled a can of blue hair spray stuff out of her bag, and we took turns giving each other racing stripes above our ears to match our uniforms. We looked good.

Finally we took the court. Our opponents, the Roadrunners, were shooting around. They were from Spokane. I hoped they'd be tired from their long trip. But they didn't look tired. They looked tall and talented.

Dad came in by himself and found a chair along the sideline. I hadn't expected him to be with anyone—with Megan—but I felt bad to see him alone. I waved to him and he waved back. His smile looked sad, even from fifty feet.

I wondered about Megan, whether she'd talked to Rex. How would he react? He didn't look like a rough-and-tumble guy, but I remembered him fearlessly getting out of his car when the bad guys were harassing me. Would he threaten Megan? She wasn't the only other one who knew his secret—I knew, Dad knew, and Lisa knew—but would that matter to Rex if he thought his whole life was about to be ruined?

But I couldn't think about Megan and Rex—or even Dad—now.

"We don't know a lot about this team," Duncan said when we gathered at our bench. "We haven't played 'em, we haven't seen 'em."

"So you just need to worry about what *you* do," Jimmy said. "You need to execute. Offensively, defensively, on the boards."

"We're the *Sorcerers,*" Autumn said.

"Sorcerers," DJ said. "On three."

We counted to three. "Sorcerers!" The yell, even in the huge building, exploded from our little circle. I got a chill up my spine, a charge in my heart. I wanted to be in, playing, battling, but as usual I'd begin the game on the bench. I'd cheer, though, as loud as I could.

DJ got the tip to Vanessa, who looped a pass in front of Autumn. She went high for a pretty layup.

They broke our press but missed an outside shot. We rebounded and took off. Rachel missed a shot, but DJ tipped it in.

The Roadrunners scored; we answered with seven straight points. They called time.

The coaches sent the starters back out with new instructions: take off the press, put on the trap, go to a zone.

We trapped, Rachel pressuring their point guard, Vanessa, DJ, and Autumn strung out behind her, and Ashley patrolling deep. Autumn and Rachel forced a bad pass and DJ got it. She fed Vanessa, who scored. We went to other things: zone press, no press, zone defense, man-to-man. With two minutes to go in the quarter, we were up by thirteen.

Duncan sent me in.

The girl I was checking was good, but I was all over her. She forced a shot and Carley rebounded and got the ball to Cristina and we were flying, all five of us, downcourt.

Cristina took the ball to the middle and hit me with a perfect pass. I took one dribble and kissed it in off the backboard. *Right-handed,* I thought as I headed back on defense. Right-handed. Automatic.

We were ahead by sixteen at halftime. I had six points, a couple of boards, and a steal. No turnovers. One foul. The second half we got a little sloppy, a little selfish, and the coaches let us know about it. But we won, 72-50. We'd made it over the first hurdle. We weren't in a hole.

As soon as I got home I took a long shower, getting the goopy feeling and blue spray out of my hair. I washed my uniform by hand, and took it downstairs and threw it in the dryer. I'd get a fresh start the next day. I found Dad dozing off on the couch and chased him to bed.

Back upstairs, I sat on my bed in my clean sweats and waited to get tired, first with the light on, reading. Then I turned off the light and lay down, stretched, listening to the ticking of the house, thinking about my life—basketball, Lisa, Autumn, Dad, Megan, Rex, Mom. And the mysterious money. Not mysterious anymore. I'd seen the last of it, I thought, and I was glad. It was blood money, after all. *Blood money.* What would I do with it? I couldn't keep it. Not now. What would Mom have done?

I switched on my lamp and got up and put on some shoes. I needed air. I needed to get sleepy or I'd be awake all night.

Outside, the air felt cool and alive. Patches of stars hung overhead. Up and down the street, houses were mostly dark, cars sat silently, trees cast long moon shadows.

I started off, wishing for a dog. A dog would keep me company, keep me safe, give me an excuse to be out this late. But even with no dog, I had to walk. I headed toward Megan's.

The white Toyota was parked in her driveway.

Part of me wanted to stop and sneak up to a window and listen. This was a conversation I wanted to hear and at the same time didn't want to hear. Had she already told him? What was he thinking? Saying? Screaming? I didn't hear any screaming. I didn't hear anything but the rumble of my stomach, the thumping of my heart. And a moment later, a click, a door opening.

Rex stepped out of the shadows. His face was only half-lit and his eyes were hidden in dark sockets.

My feet wanted to move, but I kept them still. My mouth didn't want to move, and I didn't make it.

"A victory for the Sorcerers tonight?" he said.

I nodded, not sure he could see me in the dark. If I had a sword at my side, could he see it? "Yes."

"Good," he said. "I hear you're an awesome player. You have an awesome team."

"Thanks." I stared. This was the person who had killed my mother.

"Megan told you what happened," he said. "The whole story."

"Yes."

"I'm sorry," he said. "I know that isn't going to make a difference in your life or mine, but I wanted you to hear me say it. Every minute of the past nine years I've wanted to undo the night your mom died."

"You shouldn't have done it," I said. "You shouldn't have left us there."

"I know," he said. "I hate the person I was that night. Maybe more than you hate me. You don't have to look at the face of that person in the mirror every day and wonder if he's really changed for the better." He took a deep breath and shoved his hands into his pockets and looked up at the stars.

"I don't hate you," I said, and I realized I meant it. The person I hated was the heartless, faceless, man with six fingers I'd pictured all these years.

Rex didn't have six fingers. He had a face, and it was a good one. He seemed to have a heart.

"Thank you," he said. "I wish I could bring your mom back."

"I miss her."

"I'm going to the police tomorrow," he said. "I was thinking about doing it, even before Megan told me you'd found out. Long before. I just couldn't stomach the thought of being behind bars. But once I got back up here and saw Megan, then you and your dad living by yourselves…"

Being locked away sounded scary to me, too. And I wasn't the one facing the prospect. "How long would you be in prison?"

"Two to three years is average, I think. But I've been dodging this for so long, I don't know if the courts will be harder on me or easier. Whatever happens, I'll live with it. And then maybe I'll get on with my life. Something your mom wasn't able to do."

I nodded again. Two to three years didn't seem like much. But prison years probably weren't the same as regular years. I knew how slowly time could pass when you were miserable. I swallowed, forcing down the lump in my throat. "What about Megan?"

"I've been a curse on Megan," Rex said. "But maybe the curse is over. I've done some checking. At this point, she probably wouldn't be charged with being an accessory. Supposedly, the statute of limitations on that crime has expired."

"What's that mean?" I said.

"It means there's a limit on the number of years after a crime is committed that a suspect can be charged with the crime. Besides, she took me in that night, but she didn't lie to the police."

"Have you told Megan?" I said. "She's afraid of having to leave Dulcie."

"I told her what I thought. But I'm not a lawyer. And I don't know how much faith she has in what I think. I haven't given her much reason to have faith in me."

I could've agreed with him, but that would be like a twist of the sword. "She should talk to a lawyer," I said.

Rex nodded. "She should. We'll keep telling her that, okay?"

"Okay," I said.

"Thanks for listening, Casey," he said. "I expect I'll see you in the Final Four someday."

He stepped back into the shadows. I turned and headed for home. Behind me his engine came to life and his car backed into the street, bathing me in headlights. I waited to see it cruise past me, but it didn't. I glanced over my shoulder. The Toyota was moving up the street at my pace, a half-block back.

I kept walking, Rex's headlights showing me

the way, keeping me safe, until I got home. At my door I turned and watched his taillights disappear down the street.

Back in bed, I realized I felt sorry for Rex. Was there something wrong with me? Was I a traitor? I squinted across the dimness of my room at Inigo Montoya, unforgiving, forever on his quest, then at Mom's pictures. She was smiling out at me, not angry.

I'd carried anger like a shield for as long as I could remember. But it was heavy. I knew she would want me to lay it down.

## ❧ *17* ❧

# Collision Course

Saturday morning I rode to the gym with Dad. I told him how I'd talked to Rex.

"Next time you tell me if you're planning on leaving the house in the middle of the night, Cassandra." He'd called me *Cassandra*. His knuckles were white against the steering wheel. His voice rose. "Okay?"

"Okay," I said, in a small voice. "I'm sorry."

"You were very vulnerable out there by yourself."

"I know," I said. "You think he's gone to the police yet?"

"I would've." His voice was almost back to normal. "First thing, before it ate at me too much."

"Yeah."

"No way could I have waited *nine years.*"

"No," I said. But I wondered how brave I would've been when it came right down to it.

"He thinks Megan won't be charged?" Dad said.

"No."

Dad didn't say anything for a long moment, but I thought—or imagined—I saw his face soften just a little. "Huh," he said, finally.

I joined Vanessa and Autumn in the stands when Dad and I got to the gym. Our next opponents, the Jesters, were sitting twenty feet away, dressed in red warmups, watching the early game. The Roadrunners, the team we'd beaten the night before, were losing again, this time to the team we'd face in our second game of the day, the Mountaineers. With Brooke Lockwood dominating, the Mountaineers pulled away and won. The Roadrunners, with two losses, were already out of contention. Buried.

We went through our warmup routine, although everyone looked a little out of sync. I felt a half-step slow, a little fuzzy. My shots came up short, then long when I tried to adjust.

I hoped the funk would disappear once the game started, but it didn't. We couldn't shoot. We threw bad passes, dribbled the ball off our feet, lost it out of bounds. With three minutes to go in the first quarter, Duncan called time. The score was Jesters eleven, Sorcerers five. Embarrassing. Maybe the other girls had stuff on their minds, too.

"Carley, Cristina, Thea," Duncan said, "in for Ashley, Rachel, and Vanessa." He looked at the stat sheet. "We're two out of thirteen from the field. Part of that is shot selection, the rest is I-don't-know-what. Maybe we're gonna be snakebit this game. So let's get the ball inside, get it out on the break. And put on the full-court press with a two-one-two zone in the front court."

"You've worked hard to get here," Jimmy said, "now you gotta work hard to stay alive."

"Cut 'em off," Duncan said. "Get some steals. Make some easy shots."

"Show these girls what you're made of," Jimmy said. "Execute."

"Execute," Autumn said. "On three." We huddled and put our hands together and at DJ's three-count we screamed loud enough for the whole cavernous gym to hear: "Execute!"

We looked like a different team when we took the court. We were all over, too quick for them on the press, too big for them to force it over us. By the end of the quarter the score was even at sixteen.

I went in for Autumn, Sara went in for DJ, the other starters returned. We kept pressing with fresh bodies. A minute into the quarter, Vanessa tipped away a pass at half-court, and I grabbed it out of the air, blew past a defender with a crossover dribble from left to right, and went high for a layup. The cheers shot through me like ice water.

Vanessa slapped me five as I sprinted to my defensive position. One of their players tossed in the ball, but it was a lazy toss and I saw it coming. I dove and tipped it to Rachel who hit Vanessa on the run. From flat on my stomach I saw her put in a nice little runner with her left hand.

The Jesters' coach called time. We sprinted to the bench. My shoes didn't touch the floor.

"Let's press 'em till they solve it," Duncan said. And we did. And they didn't solve it. We were up by fifteen at the half and cruised to a twenty-two-point victory.

"You're lookin' good out there, Casey," Duncan told me as we were all leaving the gym for lunch. "We don't lose a thing when you're on the court."

"Thanks," I said. Dad was walking a few feet away and must have heard. A small grin lit his face. It was good to see.

We were back at the gym at three. Our game with the Mountaineers was at four. Down on the court, the Nightingales were crushing a team of girls who looked too slow and too small to be on the same floor with them. Twice in a row the Butterfly got the ball on the wing and exploded past three defenders to score.

"She doesn't use the backboard," Vanessa said.

"Her last basket grazed the rim," I said.

"And her shoes probably smell, too," Autumn said.

We laughed. The jitters melted away a bit. I stared at the clock: 3:15. Its face was crisscrossed with bars to protect it from stray balls. I thought about Rex. Was he behind bars by now? Would they lock him up? Had he even gone to the police? Or had he changed his mind and gone somewhere else, somewhere safe?

The game ended. As we took the court, a woman was interviewing the Butterfly in front of a TV camera. I made a mental note not to watch the news that night.

Our game started. The Mountaineers had made adjustments since our last game to try to get Brooke Lockwood the ball more often, and it worked at first. Our coaches called time, and I wondered if we'd go with the box-and-one. But they made a few small changes and sent the starters back out. With the Nightingales and their coaches in the stands, we weren't going to show anything new. We'd save the box-and-one for the Butterfly.

The little changes worked. DJ had responsibility for Brooke, but the wings—Autumn and Vanessa, then me and Thea—worked harder at getting to Brooke. She couldn't get a pass, and when she did she had two players on her, front and back.

But our outside shots weren't dropping, and when we tried to press, Brooke was able to do something—usually just a hard dribble up the middle—to break it. At halftime we were only five ahead.

"Someone needs to get in her way," Jimmy said before we went back out. "She shouldn't be able to slice through you guys like that. Take a charge if you have to."

We went back to our half-court defense. We were doing okay, but we couldn't build a lead. Carley subbed in, then Cristina and me. With a couple minutes left in the third quarter, we stuck our press back on.

Brooke got the inbounds pass and took off upcourt on the dribble, head high, looking for someone to pass to. She got around Cristina, but Vanessa was there in Brooke's path, squared up and standing strong.

Vanessa took the charge, hard.

They both went down, a tangle of arms and legs hitting the gym floor with a thud I could feel in my feet from across the court. Suddenly our part of the gym went silent, except for the referee's whistle.

The ball kicked away. Brooke rolled slowly off Vanessa and sat up, looking dazed. But Vanessa lay on her back with her leg twisted under her. Her head rolled back and forth and her fists clenched and unclenched and her chest stuttered up and down as if she was gasping for breath, or crying.

The coaches rushed out as the ref signaled an offensive foul, as Brooke got to her feet and stood, wobbly, looking down at Vanessa.

Duncan and Jimmy knelt down next to her.

A woman with an equipment bag hurried onto the court. She got down close to Vanessa's face and talked to her, then carefully eased her leg out from under her, straightening it from that ugly angle.

Gently, the coaches got her to her feet, one under each arm, their arms around her back, and carried her toward the bench. The crowd stood, the players stood. Everyone gave her a hand.

I followed along with the rest of our players. When we were almost to the bench, Vanessa looked up at Jimmy. Tears were leaking out of her eyes. "I took the charge, Jimmy," she said.

Jimmy nodded. He swallowed, hard.

The woman put a giant ice pack around Vanessa's knee, then began wrapping it. Vanessa's parents sat on either side of her, holding her hands.

Her knee, I thought. Her *knee.* All I knew about knee injuries was that they were bad news: surgery and rehab and braces and all that. I got a huge lump in my throat. I wiped at my eyes with the bottom of my jersey, pretending I was wiping off sweat.

We took the floor with Autumn subbing in for Vanessa. Brooke was back on the court for the Mountaineers, and that didn't seem fair. But she looked as if she'd had some air let out of her, and when we brought the ball downcourt and I got it into DJ at the low post, Brooke barely contested the shot. We were up by eight.

I looked over at the bench. Vanessa had a towel over her head and a wrap the size of a bowling ball around her knee. She gave me the thumps-up sign and a small grin.

We were half mad and half in shock, and it seemed to be a combination that worked for us: fire and ice. We put on the press, full court man-to-man, and they didn't respond this time. We were everywhere, contesting everything, making steals, blocking shots. DJ cleaned nearly everything off the boards, and Carley got the leftovers.

The coaches kept me in until we were halfway through the fourth quarter, until I was dragging, until we were up by nineteen. Then I sat next to Vanessa and watched us put the game away. We'd won another one. We'd made it through another day. We were two games away from Iowa. But we didn't feel like laughing. We couldn't look at Vanessa and even smile.

I rode home with Dad. "I love watching you on this team," he said.

"I love playing on this team."

We were full of chatter for a while. He was proud of the way I'd played, and I bounced a lot of stuff off him about the games and Vanessa's injury.

Finally we got quiet. He put in a CD, and soft music filled the car. "Do you think Megan and Dulcie will come to the games tomorrow?" I said.

Dad didn't answer right away. He glanced over at me and moved his eyes back to the road. "It's possible."

"Can you call her when we get home?"

He handed me his cell phone. "Go ahead."

I didn't take it. "I think you should. It won't mean as much if I call."

"I wouldn't know what to say."

"Tell her you understand."

"I'm not sure I do."

"Oh."

Dad turned the music up, then down.

"Do *you* understand?" he said.

"I don't know," I said. "But I could tell her I do. Then maybe someday I would."

He smiled, sad-eyed. "Your mom was like that, you know. Understanding. It's never been that easy for me. It's always taken me time."

"That's okay," I said, and I left it at that. He hadn't made any promises, but he hadn't closed the door, either.


Megan said hello on the first ring, sounding wide-awake.

"It's me," I said, settling back on my bed. "Sorry it's so late."

"Casey." She made my name sound like a prayer. "It's so nice to hear your voice."

"I've been busy," I said.

"I know. Did you win?"

"All three so far. But Vanessa got hurt. Bad."

"Oh, no."

I told her about our games, the teams we'd played, our team, how I'd done. I stayed on the subject of basketball, not sure what to say about the rest. But I'd called her. Didn't that say something?

Maybe not enough. "Can you come to the tournament tomorrow?" I said.

There was a pause at the other end. "You want me to?"

"And Dulcie. Bring Dulcie." I wasn't quite as worried now about Megan being jailed, but if it happened, I knew where Dulcie would have a home. I loved Dulcie.

"What about your dad?"

"He won't care. He said I could call you." Which was true, as far as it went.

"Let me think about it, okay?" she said. "You don't need distractions tomorrow."

"You wouldn't be. I'd play better if you guys were there."

"We'll see," she said. When Megan said, "We'll see," it usually meant no. But I didn't want to beg.

We talked for a while longer before we said good-bye. The last thing she said to me was this: "I love you, Casey. Always. No matter what."

"Me, too," I said.

## ❧ *18* ❧

# So Ready for the Nightingales

**O**ur first game on Sunday, the final day, was at 1:00. Duncan wanted us there by 11:30.

By 10:15 Dad and I were sitting in the Jeep with the Mukilteo ferry rumbling along beneath us. He was snoozing, pretending to read the *Seattle Times*. I had the comics, unread on my lap.

My window was down; a salty breeze and reflected sunshine and the sounds of seagulls swept in. I couldn't have felt more awake.

I came to a decision. "Dad?"

"Uh-huh?" He opened his eyes and looked at me.

"I know what I want to do with the money."

"Your money?"

"Rex's money. It's *blood* money. I don't want it."

"You've thought of a good use for it?"

"Dulcie," I said. "Dulcie should get half. She's

Rex's daughter. She'll need money for college and stuff, even if he's giving her some already."

"Good," Dad said. He waited a moment. "The other half?"

"When I was at Autumn's school—Jefferson—I went into the library. The place is hurting, Dad. It practically echoes in there. I want to give the rest of the money to the Jefferson library so they can buy books for the kids."

Dad smiled and gave me a hug. "Okay," he said. "We'll figure out how we can do that." He eased back, hands on my shoulders, and looked in my eyes.

"What?" I said.

"I think I see a little more light in there already," he said. "This decision of yours—it's going to help us move on. I know it is. We'll be able to remember your mom's life without the constant reminder of her death."

He was right. I felt like a weight had lifted. The money had become a burden; now it wasn't. I nodded. I breathed in the cool air, deep, and let it out.


The Rattlers were a tall team. To show us how tall, they jogged around the whole court before they got into their warmup routine. I wished Vanessa was there; she would have given them a hard time for invading our territory.

With a few minutes to go before game time,

the coaches led us over to a corner.

"You're all wondering about Vanessa," Duncan said. "I hope to see her later, maybe for the second game if there is one. But she's in pain, she's swollen up, and she didn't sleep last night, according to her folks. The docs think she's got some ligament and cartilage damage, and that she'll need surgery."

He looked around at our tight little circle—too little, without Vanessa.

"So if she shows up today," said Jimmy, "it won't be to play ball."

"Which means we all need to work harder," Duncan said. "Because you don't lose a player like Vanessa without making adjustments."

"It also means we need to replace her in the starting lineup," Jimmy said.

He looked at me. At *me.*

"Casey," Duncan said, "we're gonna start you this game. We're gonna see if you give us as much energy as a starter as you do coming off the bench."

I glanced at Thea. She was the other wing, she'd been with the team longer. I thought she'd be the new starter. I thought she'd be upset if she wasn't. But she smiled at me. A real smile. "Okay," I said. "Thanks."

"We're down to three wings," Jimmy said. "You're all gonna get more playing time."

Duncan pulled out his clipboard and marker. He

took a knee and we knelt down with him. "Let's see how we're gonna play this team," he said.

We went over the plan. Play tough half-court man-to-man, hit the boards, run the offense, take high-percentage shots, fast break when we could. Execute. With the possibility of another game in a few hours, the coaches wanted us to hold off on the press. They didn't want us to blow all our energy on the first game and have nothing left for the second.

"But if we don't win the first one," Jimmy said, "there's not gonna be a second one."

We took the court for the tip-off, slapping hands with the Rattlers. It felt good to be starting, except I didn't feel good about the reason: Vanessa's injury. I had to play well enough so everyone wouldn't wish *she* was out there instead of *me*.

I'd only seen DJ lose one tip, and that was to the flying girl. She didn't lose this one. Autumn got the ball and we got into our zone offense, working it, reversing it, sending cutters through. Ashley, double-teamed at the low post, fired the ball out to me. I swished it through and headed downcourt, smiling.

The Rattlers scored inside. Autumn missed a shot, but DJ rebounded and put it in. They missed and we rebounded, and Rachel hit me with a nice pass on the left wing and I let the ball fly. Swish.

They scored. Autumn hit a three-pointer, then a

two from outside. They scored again. We missed a shot, then missed the rebound shot. DJ got another rebound and rifled it out to me under pressure. I put it up but it rimmed out.

A quick downcourt pass, and their point guard was flying toward the hoop with the ball. From out of nowhere came Autumn to block the shot. It sailed out of bounds. She came down smiling big, holding her hand high to slap ours.

DJ stole the inbounds pass and whipped the ball to Rachel, who got it to me, who fed it to Ashley for a nice layup. Their coach stood, yelling directions. They got a girl loose and scored on a baseline jumper.

We maintained a slim lead. With fifteen seconds to go in the half, we were up by three, playing for the last shot. I'd been out, but now I was back in. Autumn hit me with a nice pass at the top of the key. One of their big players picked me up, overplaying my left. Without thinking, I faked left, got her leaning, and went right. Someone lunged at me from the left but I stayed right, went up, and banked it in, right-handed. It felt natural, it felt good.

The horn blew. It was halftime.

We still hadn't pressed or trapped, and the coaches kept us in our half-court defense to start the second half. But by the end of the third quarter we were up by only four.

"Okay," Jimmy said. "Starting five on the floor."

"It's their ball," Duncan said. "I want a full-court zone press. Fall back in a two-three zone if they break it."

"Don't *let* 'em break the press," Jimmy said.

Duncan smiled. "We'll mix in the trap, too. I'll let you know."

We set up in our press formation. "Energy!" Duncan shouted, and I got into a half-crouch, waiting to break on the ball. They got it in, but Rachel was too quick for their point guard, who let herself get channeled to the sideline, where Autumn picked her up. One of their players cut to the center of the court, but I shadowed her and when the pass came, high and looping, I stepped in front of her and got it. I had clear sailing for an easy layup.

We set up in the press again. This time Autumn stole the ball and hit Rachel going to the hoop for another two. They tried a long pass downcourt and DJ snapped it up. Autumn scored inside. And she was fouled.

Their coach called time. Suddenly we were up by ten.

"The next three opportunities, go to the trap," Duncan told us. "Then back to the press, probably. Jimmy will call it. Just listen."

Listen? How could we help it? Jimmy's voice could fill that big gym.

Autumn missed her foul shot. They made a

three. DJ muscled in a shot for us.

We backed up into our trap formation. The ballhandler got trapped near the sideline, picked up her dribble, and threw the ball out of bounds.

Carley, Cristina, and Thea came in. DJ and I stayed. Cristina missed an outside shot but Carley went high to tip it in. We were rolling. I could feel it.

With two minutes to go we had a fifteen-point lead, and the coaches took off the pressure and subbed. I sat, tired, but not worn out. I had a lot of energy for the next game. There *would be* a next game.

I looked at the spectators lined up in chairs along the court, I looked in the stands. No Megan. No Dulcie. No Lisa. And no Vanessa. When Dad saw me looking, he waved. On the court next to us, the Nightingales were winning with less than a minute to go, but only by nine.

We won, 62-51. We were happy, smiling, the coaches were happy and trying not to smile. We weren't celebrating. "Close doesn't count for Iowa," Duncan said.

Our next game—the championship game!—was at 4:30, so we had an hour or so to eat something light and get back to the gym. It wouldn't take me that long. My stomach was already getting ready—shrinking and knotting—and I didn't think I'd have much room, even for a snack.

Autumn stopped me on my way out of the gym. "You hungry?" she said.

"Not really."

"Good. We took a vote. We're all meeting at the Starbucks at Juanita Beach. Energy food, baby."

"What did your dad say?" I asked.

"He said, 'Whatever works.'"

It was a five-minute ride to the coffee shop. We walked in as a team, sweaty, hair on the loose or hidden under ball caps. Mine was ponytailed but barely under control. Our parents straggled in behind us.

I felt eyes on me as we lined up at the counter. Some of the tables were occupied. "Hey, Sorcerers!" someone called from across the room. Four high-school-age guys at a table by the window. One of them was Noah. "Good game, girls!" he said.

"Thanks!" we said, not quite in unison.

While the line grew shorter in front of us, Autumn kept glancing out at the parking lot.

"Mom's meeting us here," she said. "She's going across the street first to get something."

"What?"

"You'll see."

We got our drinks and joined the other girls at a couple of tables near the window. We were close to the boys but not so close that we'd have to talk to them. Just as we sat, Mrs. Hopkins walked in.

She came over and emptied a bag on our table.

Face paint. Two small brushes. "I'm the artist," she said, sitting down. "Now I just need some customers."

"Line up," Autumn said. "We're going to do a V on everyone's cheek."

"For Vanessa?" I said.

"For Vanessa," Autumn said. "And victory."

We took turns sitting in front of Autumn's mom. She put a fancy purple V with a sparkly gold outline on everybody's right cheek. She was quick, and as soon as she was done, we all crowded into the bathroom to check ourselves out in the mirror. We looked stunning. We went outside in the sun and Mrs. Hopkins took our picture. We were so ready for the Nightingales.

# ~ *19* ~

## All-or-Nothin' Time

Inside the gym, the crowd had grown. The gym had been rearranged. Baskets stood on both ends of the big court, bleachers were out on both sides. The tournament was down to one game; we needed only one place to play it. At one corner of the court, a KOMO reporter was talking to her cameraman. A couple of guys carrying cameras stood nearby with a man and woman holding notebooks. Newspaper reporters.

My stomach clenched like a fist. I hadn't expected this.

The coaches sent us out on the court to shoot around while they huddled over strategies. They both looked as nervous—Duncan chewing on a pencil, Jimmy tugging and re-tugging at his ear—as I felt. But some of my nervousness went away once

I'd tightened up my shoes and got my hands on a ball.

The Nightingales came in, making their grand entrance, looking like they expected—no, *deserved*—the attention they were getting. At the rear of their little parade walked Teresa Bonilla—la Mariposa—talking to the woman newspaper reporter. Teresa looked loose and relaxed and sure of herself.

I felt myself getting angry. I told myself that by the end of the game none of the reporters would be talking to Teresa Bonilla. They'd be talking to Autumn and DJ and Rachel and Duncan and Jimmy. And maybe even me.

The clock ticked down toward 4:30. We started our warmup routine, looking good with our V-for-Vanessa cheeks. Even the coaches liked them. But Vanessa was still a no-show. And so was Megan. Sitting in the stands among the other parents, Dad looked pretty lonely.

The Nightingales were warming up, running layups from two lines, and now Noah and his buddies, standing high in the bleachers, started a chant whenever the Butterfly was about to get the ball: "Dunk it! Dunk it! Dunk it!"

She pretended not to hear them. But they kept it up, and pretty soon she glanced over in their direction and gave them a little grin and they got louder. Still she didn't try to dunk. What fourteen-year-old girl could?

Finally she flew in from the left side and went extra high, just finger-rolling the ball over the front of the rim. The boys cheered and whooped, and I wondered if they would be making that much noise for us once the game started. Whose side were they on, anyway?

"Infants!" Autumn said as she got into line behind me. "I don't even *know* that boy!"

Jimmy called us to the sideline. Duncan was schmoozing with the refs, trying to earn some nice-guy points. He hurried over as soon as we sat.

"Tops on our list is Teresa," he said. "We've decided to go with the box-and-one defense right from the start. If it bombs, we'll adjust."

"You're the 'one,' Autumn," Jimmy said. "We thought that would be Vanessa's spot, but she's not here now. You'll have help, though."

Duncan showed us the defense on his clipboard. "Rachel and Casey, you've got the outside corners, DJ and Ashley are inside. You need to take care of your area, but be aggressive in helping out on Teresa. If she comes anywhere near you, or even if she looks like she's thinking about it, you need to challenge her."

I was starting. And I'd be out in the area where the Butterfly liked to set up. I needed to give Autumn all the help I could.

"Go all out all the time," Duncan said as the

horn sounded. "We got fresh bodies to throw at 'em when you get tired."

We stood in our huddle and shouted out a cheer: "Vanessa!"

And almost on cue, she hobbled into the gym, on crutches, with her mom and dad. I didn't know if she could see the V's yet, but she smiled, wide.

We checked in with the scorer. As we headed back, I glanced toward the gym door.

Megan was walking in. With Dulcie on one side and Lisa on the other. They'd come.

Everyone I wanted to be here, *was* here.

Even Mom. I couldn't see her, but I felt her eyes on me.

We stood while a high school girl sang the national anthem. Then the introductions began. First their nonstarters, then ours. Then the announcer alternated, one of their starters, one of ours, and we ran out onto the court and slapped hands with the Nightingale who went out with us. I went last, hearing in my head the echoes of the announcer's voice saying CASEY WILDE, and when I got out there, floating, in front of all those people, the Butterfly was there, waiting to slap five with me.

"Good luck, Casey," she said as our hands brushed.

"You, too," I said, "Teresa."

The crowd cheered as the announcer introduced Vanessa. She came out on her crutches with the rest of the team walking close. The cheers grew louder as Vanessa looked around at our faces, the V's. Tears filled her eyes. Then the sound faded. Half the team went back to the bench while we stayed on the court. Time for business.

Teresa out-jumped DJ for the opening tip and raced downcourt, looking for a pass.

"Man!" their point guard called, dribbling, watching Teresa cut through our defense and Autumn stick to her like a wet shirt. But the rest of us settled into our positions; we weren't playing man-to-man.

"One-three-one!" their coach yelled. They scrambled into a zone offense as the shot clock wound down. With a couple seconds to go, they threw up an ugly shot that clanged off the rim.

Ashley rebounded and whipped an outlet pass to Rachel, who got the ball to me. I bounced it past Teresa's long fingers to Autumn, who made the shot and got fouled. She slapped me five, then calmly sank the free-throw.

They hurried the ball into front court, still trying to solve our defense. Finally the Butterfly got the ball, shed Autumn, and went up for a shot. DJ leaped and got a piece of the ball, and Teresa's arm. The whistle blew. Teresa sank both free throws.

Their coach called time. "Caja y uno," Teresa said to their point guard as the Nightingales headed to their bench.

The point guard returned a blank look.

"Box-and-one," Teresa said with disgust.

"They know what we're running," I said when we sat. "Teresa figured it out."

"Knowing what we're running isn't the same as knowing what to do about it," Duncan said.

We got close to the bench so Vanessa could join in the cheer: "Execute!"

They came out in a press, but DJ passed me the ball as I flashed down the right side. The Butterfly cut me off but I pulled up and shot. Nothing but net.

We set up the box-and-one. Teresa was running Autumn ragged, but she wasn't losing her. And every time the flying girl got near our *caja,* she had everyone's attention.

She was the Butterfly, but we were the net.

They put up a shot. Ashley had position for the rebound, but Teresa rose up and snatched it, then went up high for a shot that banked in. The whistle blew. Foul, on Autumn. "Te-reee-sa Bo-neee-ya!" the announcer sing-songed.

"Don't reach!" Duncan yelled.

Teresa sank the free throw, tying the score.

For the next three minutes we traded baskets. We were even at eleven when Autumn committed foul number two. Thea, subbing for Autumn, was the "one" now.

The quarter ended with the Nightingales up by

three. Carley, Sara, and Cristina checked in for me, Ashley, and Rachel. Autumn stayed on the bench.

We stuck with the box-and-one. Carley, who was quick and big, took over the Butterfly chase. And with the help of the rest of our players, she shut down Teresa—except for two foul shots—for the first three minutes or so. Finally, the Nightingales' coach gave her a rest.

Both teams kept battling. The half ended with us trailing, 38-36. Just before halftime, Autumn got called for her third foul. On our bench, both coaches held their heads.

On my way off the floor, I glanced up at the stands. Dad was still in his spot, alone. Up above him, ten rows and a world away, sat Megan and Dulcie and Lisa.

The coaches herded us outside and went over the stats. Despite our defense, Teresa had eighteen points.

Duncan looked at Autumn, then Carley. "We can't afford more fouls for you two. And all of you need to do a better job of finding each other on offense."

"Amen," Vanessa said, suspended on her crutches. "Get some assists. Fly around out there. This is for Iowa." She had a big sparkly S on her cheek. For Sorcerers.

"Still comfortable with the box-and-one?" Jimmy said.

We nodded.

"Carley," Duncan said. "You did a good job on her. Take her to start the half."

We went back to the bench and huddled up.

"Iowa," Vanessa said. "On three." And we shouted out the name of Mom's school.

Each team got a basket to start the half, but on the Nightingales' next possession, Carley, trying to stop Teresa, picked up her third foul.

Duncan called time. We went to the bench.

"We got foul trouble," Jimmy said. "We need another candidate for chaser."

"I've got no fouls," I said. "None. Zero. Let me have her."

Duncan grinned. "Okay, rookie. Give her all you got."

I made her work for it, but Teresa caught the inbounds pass. I forced her to the baseline. She dribbled back out, looking inside, but our defense wouldn't soften, and she whipped the ball crosscourt.

"I'll wear you out, Casey," she said, breaking toward the key. But in the key I had help. The wing tried to force the ball into her, but Autumn leaped high and snatched it and floated a pass over the last defender to Rachel, who made a driving layup. We were tied.

The quarter clock ticked away. We traded baskets. Teresa was running me all over, but I was hanging in there. She made one shot but missed two.

The coaches subbed. I stayed in, tired but not about to show it, hanging with the Butterfly. On offense I got a break. Teresa was focused on Autumn, who had sunk three outside shots in a row.

Just before the quarter ended, Teresa drove for a layup. I smacked the ball but hammered her. We crashed to the floor out of bounds. The whistle blew.

The coaches—both sides—stood, looking nervous. Teresa got to her feet and helped me up. "Good foul, Casey."

"Good move, Teresa." I had one foul now. Four to go. I'd use them all if I had to.

She smiled. She made one free throw, then missed. The horn blew. One quarter to go. Sorcerers fifty-four, Nightingales fifty-three.

As I trudged off the floor I looked again at the stands. Dad was gone from his spot. When I spotted him a moment later, he wasn't alone anymore. He was ten rows higher, standing next to Megan. I saw him say something to her. I saw her nod.

My legs didn't feel heavy now, my lungs didn't feel empty. I was ready for anything.

We sat while the coaches knelt. "If they rest her, let's go to the trap until she comes back," Duncan said. "Otherwise, we'll stick with our junk defense."

Jimmy looked at me. "Heck of a job, Casey. We're gonna give you a little rest. A minute, maybe. Then you're back on her. Autumn, you got her till then."

Thea checked in for me. I sat, not wanting to sit, as my team went back out like warriors. Vanessa sat next to me.

Suddenly I felt her eyes on me. "I couldn't have done better," she said.

"Thanks," I said. "But I wish you were playing."

"Yeah," she said.

We had the ball first. DJ scored inside. We were up by three.

The Butterfly, at high post now, got a lob pass from the point guard and spun away from Autumn. She snaked past Ashley and dropped in a little floater.

Thea found Autumn with a pass to the baseline. Swish. Three points. Up by four.

They came back and slipped the ball into Teresa, who pivoted for the hoop with Autumn on her hip and Carley moving to cut her off. Teresa went up. Her shot rattled through. The whistle blew. Number forty-four, the ref signaled. Carley again. Four fouls.

Sara went in for Carley. The Butterfly sank her foul shot. Our lead was down to one.

The coaches called time.

Duncan knelt, scribbling frantically. "Casey, in for Thea. Rachel, in for Cristina. Here's what we're gonna do." He showed us the diagram he'd markered on the clipboard. "Triangle-and-two," he said. "Like the box-and-one, but we've got Casey back on Teresa and Autumn on their point guard, in her face. We can't let her make that easy pass. Rachel, you've got this zone around the free throw line, DJ and Sara, you're deep."

"You guys in the triangle have a lot of area to cover," Jimmy said, "plus you still have to help out on Teresa."

Duncan glanced up at the clock. "You've got less than seven minutes left."

Rachel got me the ball. My man was guarding me too close. I jab-stepped and crossed over to my right hand and lost her. Before anyone could react, I was in the air, laying it in. We were up by three and about to try a new defense.

Their point guard, hounded by Autumn, looked frantically for Teresa, but I was in the way. She got off a pass to a post player, who passed back out for a hurried shot by a wing. It went in. Ouch.

Autumn drove, then pulled up and whipped the ball to Sara underneath. Sara's shot rimmed out. I missed the putback, and the Nightingales grabbed the ball and got it to Teresa, but before she could get past me, I fouled her. Their inbounds pass bounced off a Nightingales shin and went out. Carley and Ashley came in for Sara and Rachel. Autumn moved to point.

We missed shots the next two times downcourt, but the Nightingales couldn't take advantage. Finally DJ scored inside. Up by three.

Having Carley in the game helped defensively. I was able to play Teresa tight and have Carley back me up inside. But with three minutes to go, Teresa got by me and Carley tried to stop her. She got a piece of the ball, but the whistle blew.

She'd fouled out.

Thea checked in and Carley headed for the bench. The crowd gave her a big hand. Wiping at her eyes, she sat down next to Jimmy, who draped his arm around her shoulders and gave her a fatherly squeeze.

The Butterfly swished both free throws. We were ahead but barely, 63-62.

Autumn tried to drive inside, but Teresa fouled her. We inbounded the ball underneath, but couldn't get off a shot. DJ got the ball to Thea, who passed it to me, and with the shot clock ticking down I launched a shot. It went in and out. The Nightingales rebounded and fired the ball downcourt, where Teresa chased it down. She flew to the hoop and scored, and the announcer sang out her name.

We were down by one.

The coaches called time. They were standing, heads together, as we got to the bench. I sat and looked up at the clock: two minutes, fifteen seconds. Anyone's game. Dad and Megan were still together. They looked as tense as I felt.

"Okay," Duncan said. "We're gonna go with a straight-up man defense, full-court, with a smaller lineup. So along with DJ we're gonna have nothing but wings and guards—Autumn, Casey, Rachel, and Cristina. That means you're all gonna have to play bigger."

"You got two minutes to fly around," Jimmy said. "Use all your fuel."

"Autumn, you take Teresa," Duncan said. "Play her tight. It's all-or-nothin' time."

"Go get her, Hops," Jimmy said.

"That should give you a little more freedom, Casey," Duncan said. "Look to get open, look for your shot. And this is for everyone—help out Autumn."

We tossed in the ball, Rachel to Cristina, then back to Rachel to set it up. I was on the right post, low, but I moved out to get more maneuvering space. The Butterfly was on Autumn, tight.

We ran through our offense. We couldn't afford a turnover. Finally Cristina got a nice entry pass into DJ, who turned and head-faked and rose up for an easy shot. But from out of nowhere the Butterfly soared in. She didn't block the shot but she caused DJ to alter it and the ball bounced twice on the rim and fell off.

They grabbed the rebound and held on under pressure, moving upcourt. We were everywhere, but we couldn't get our hands on the ball.

They ran their offense, trying to isolate Teresa, but Autumn was shadowing and nudging and windmilling and making it tough for her. Finally they set a screen and got their superstar the ball. DJ cut her off but she whistled a pass to DJ's man, open under the basket. I couldn't react fast enough. We were down by three.

Rachel hurried the ball upcourt. She drove inside, and when the Butterfly challenged her she lofted the ball toward Autumn, who was cutting toward the basket. But the pass was too high. It sailed out.

Nightingales' ball. Our chances were fading, but they weren't gone yet. I found my man as we put on our press. I rode her, hard. Their point guard fired a pass toward the Butterfly, but Autumn knocked it out of bounds.

They inbounded the ball to Teresa. Autumn wouldn't give an inch. The Butterfly forced it inside, but I was ready. I tapped it to Autumn. Teresa moved with her, channeling her away from the basket, but Autumn threw me a perfect pass. I headed for the hoop, one defender to beat. At the top of the key she tried to force me right, overplaying my left hand, and I crossed over, left to right, and blew by her. I went up strong and sank the layup. I glanced up at the scoreboard as the gym filled with noise.

Nightingales sixty-six, Sorcerers sixty-five. Twenty seconds to go.

We pressed, all out. The Butterfly grabbed the ball and looked to get it inbounds. She whipped it to a Nightingale in backcourt, and I thought *foul her,* but before Cristina could get there, the girl had rifled the ball toward the half-court circle and one of their tall players.

And DJ. She stepped in front of the girl, tipped the ball, and came down with it.

She found me with a pass. I turned toward our hoop, knowing the clock was dying.

In front of me, forty feet away, was our basket. Between the basket and me was a Nightingale, closing in. Beyond her I saw Autumn, breaking toward the hoop, but on her hip, too close, was the Butterfly.

I had only one option: get to the basket in a hurry. I drove, heart pounding. My defender challenged me, but I crossed over left to right, got her leaning, then crossed over again, right to left, and accelerated past her, deadly.

But now I had a new obstacle: the Butterfly,

drifting away from Autumn, edging toward me, trying to cover both of us. I had a decision to make: shoot or pass.

But Teresa made my decision for me. Suddenly she stormed out and met me at the free throw line. I picked up my dribble and went up, high. She went up, higher. And I slipped a bounce-pass under her outstretched arm. Right-handed.

In slow motion Autumn gathered in the ball. And pivoted. And put it up off the board. In slow motion the ball dropped cleanly through the basket. The announcer's voice, low and drawn-out, growled, "Au-tummmn HOP-kinnns!"

The horn wailed. Noise erupted. Autumn leaped in the air and leaped again, laughing, running toward me. My feet wouldn't move. The Butterfly turned and walked away, head down. Teammates and coaches surrounded us. Carley was crying. Vanessa was half in the knot of arms and legs and bodies, half out, trying not to get crushed. Our V's were smeared and running down our cheeks.

"Iowa!" someone said, then two or three people said it: "Iowa!" And in an instant it was all of us. "I-o-wa! I-o-wa! I-o-wa!" The chant spread up to the stands, to our fans. "I-o-wa! I-o-wa! I-o-wa!"

Through watery eyes I tried to focus on the faces in the crowd. I found Dad, standing next to Megan still, sandwiched by Dulcie and Lisa.

Lisa held a piece of cardboard. On it was scrawled in big letters, "I'm going!" They were all shouting and clapping and swaying back and forth. They smiled and waved. I waved back.

Both hands.

We got teary-eyed congratulations from the Nightingales, and ribbons, and a big trophy that said Washington State Champions. Autumn and DJ got named to the all-tournament team. I got picked for the second team. Me. Casey Wilde. From Whidbey Island. What would Mom have thought of her girl?

I squinted my eyes half-closed and looked up at the farthest, highest, corner of the stands, where the light was weak, where murk and shadows made things possible. I imagined her standing there, smiling, proud, remembering her teams and teammates and wishing she could be with them, and with me, again.

But she *was* with me. She always would be.